SHADOW LOST

THE SHADOW ACCORDS

D.K. HOLMBERG

ASH PUBLISHING

CHAPTER 1

THE EMPTINESS OF THE VILLAGE STRUCK CARTHENNE REL.

It was more than how no one moved along the streets, or—more surprisingly—how no one greeted them when they rowed the small dinghy to the rocky shore to purchase supplies. It was even more than the way the two smaller sailing ships anchored out from shore bobbed on the waves, the only sign of life she had seen from them.

This was a feeling, as if the entirety of the village had simply vanished.

"I'm not liking this, Carth."

Guya's hand loosely gripped his knife, but he left it sheathed and swayed slightly, as if he were still at the helm of his ship. There was no reason for him to pull it free, but Carth wouldn't have blamed him had he unsheathed it. She nearly pulled her own knife free of its sheath.

"Me neither," she said.

Guya paused in what would be a tall grassy plain when

the weather was warmer, now dried and trampled. The only color Carth noticed was a flash of maroon on the opposite side of the clearing. The coppery hint in the salty air was enough for her to know what it was.

"You knew, didn't you?" Guya asked. He scanned the clearing, taking in everything around them before letting his gaze settle on Carth. There was a weight in it, and under different circumstances—and before she had come to know him—it would have been intimidating. Now, there was only a sense of concern from him as he looked upon her with his dark eyes.

"You saw the ships the same I did."

Guya grunted. "Didn't think you would have known what that meant."

Carth smiled grimly. "Just because I'm not a sailor like you doesn't mean I'm not able to pick up on what's happening. Slashed sails, scorched hull, nothing else moving. That tells me they'd been attacked."

"Piracy," Guya said.

"That looked like something more than piracy." In the months since they'd left Wesjan, just sailing blindly, letting her and Dara grow more comfortable with serving as his mates, they had seen signs of piracy more than once. Often enough that Carth knew the signs of a ship that had been claimed by others. What floated out from shore wasn't the result of piracy. It was the result of an attack.

"Maybe."

"Look around you, Guya. Where is everyone? There's no one here."

"Maybe they left."

Carth shot Guya a look, which he ignored.

The village was isolated, located on the end of what looked to be a long peninsula. Access to the sea and the ships that now were useless would have been essential for survival.

"They didn't leave. Something chased them out."

"Or worse," Guya said.

Carth nodded. That was more likely, especially with the blood she had seen.

"Let's see if there's anything else we can find," she said.

Guya nodded.

They made their way from building to building. The style here was different than in other places they had visited over the months, with most built from thick rock stacked and somehow sealed together, and long reeds used to thatch the roofs.

When they had made their way through the village—it hadn't taken long, since the village wasn't large—Carth and Guya stood on an outcropping of rock looking out over the sea. The water was violent here and crashed along the rock, spray filling the air. Neither of them spoke at first.

"There's dried meat and some grain," Guya said softly.

Carth nodded. She'd seen the same.

"No one here, was there?"

Carth shook her head. No one was here, and with the amount of their possessions the villagers had left behind, it was clear they hadn't left on their own. This had been an attack. There was too much blood splattered through too many of the buildings for it to be anything else.

"What do you want to do now?" Guya asked.

"Load up what we can. Take whatever might be valuable so we can trade it in the next port."

"Lonsyn," Guya said.

Lonsyn would be a few days' sailing from here, long enough that they would need the supplies they gathered. It didn't feel right taking what was here, but then, they had intended to sail in for trade. Everything they had on the dinghy would end up back on the ship with them.

"What are you going to tell her?"

Carth thought about what to tell Dara. She had a sensitive heart, especially when it came to things like this, and even more so after what she'd been through before Carth had met her, and then again in the time since.

"I don't think we tell her anything," Carth decided.

"She's going to ask why we have the same supplies back on board."

Carth nodded. Dara was observant. It made her a more capable ally, but she'd been hurt often enough that she didn't always see everything the same way she might have. Especially since the Hjan had used her, forcing her to attack, the woman had changed. Anyone would. Carth wanted to keep her from that as much as she could.

"We'll hide them."

"We can't keep hiding from things, Carth. You don't have a plan yet, do you?"

"I thought we were sailing."

"Sailing. That's what we've been doing, but it feels like you've been running."

She frowned. "What would I have to run from?"

"You're powerful, I don't deny that, but since we finished with that business in Wesjan, you've been doing nothing but staying clear of what you need to face head-on."

"And what's that? I helped forge an alliance between two factions who've been warring for longer than most know. I convinced the Hjan that they couldn't continue to attack, pulling them into the accords. And there's peace in the north."

Or there should be. This village was a part of the north, but that didn't change the fact something had happened here. This might not have been the same as what she'd seen when the Hjan had attacked, and it might not have involved the A'ras, or the Reshian, but there was unrest here the same way there had been in other places.

"There's peace, and we've been making certain that it holds. But we've seen no other sign of the Hjan, and the A'ras have returned to Nyaesh while the Reshian…"

He didn't need to finish. The Reshian had disappeared, and with them, her father. There was nowhere for her to search for answers, no way for her to understand why he'd left her in Nyaesh, letting her think that he was dead along with her mother.

Without her telling him, Guya had known. Of course, he had known. They had traveled together long enough that even when she'd tried deceiving herself, she hadn't deceived him.

"We could travel south…"

He'd made a similar suggestion several times, and each time, Carth had refused, her answer the same: eventually. She suspected she would *need* to travel south, and would need to understand where the Hjan came from, but she wouldn't do it until she felt settled with what had happened in the north.

"Not south. Not yet. We haven't seen any sign of the Reshian," Carth said. "And we've sailed pretty much all the way around the north. There's been nothing."

"There's one place we haven't visited," Guya said.

She nodded. "We haven't. You told me it was empty. That there wasn't anything left of Ih-lash since the Hjan attacked."

"I haven't visited Ih-lash for years, Carth. The last time I was there, they were as prosperous as ever. It was a place I loved to trade. Always good coin, and never a shady deal. No one could get away with anything, but now that I see how you use the shadows, I wonder if maybe they knew what was planned before anyone attempted it."

"But the Hjan attacked it."

"That's the rumor."

Carth smiled. "I've heard it often enough that I take it as more than rumor, Guya. It wasn't only you, but also the A'ras, and they have the same ability to search out information."

"Spies, you mean."

Carth shrugged. "They didn't call themselves that…"

"But they were spies."

"I don't know that I can visit Ih-lash," Carth said. "I don't have much in the way of memories, but what I do have…"

They were good memories, what she could recall of Ih-lash. It was a time when her parents had been happy, a time before they had run from city to city, when they had simply *been*. Carth no longer remembered what that was like. For almost as long as she could recall, she had moved. Even in Nyaesh, there had been movement. First from the docks to the palace, and then it had been the movement of trying to attain higher levels within the A'ras, always competing and never getting to where she wanted.

"Don't you think you ought to try to find him?"

She noted that he suggested only her. Guya hadn't shared what his plans were, but she suspected he wanted to return to the south eventually. She wasn't ready for that. "What do you think we're after?"

He grunted. "Not finding your father. You need a kind of closure no one else is going to give you, Carth. Not searching the seas like we've been, not if we were to return you to Nyaesh, not even if we brought you back to Odian."

She smiled at that. "There's nothing in Odian."

"I thought you told me there was your master of Tsatsun."

"Ras might not even be there anymore. After the Hjan took him away, he might not have returned."

She had considered returning, though. If only to learn more about him, and to understand what he might have intended. As a master of Tsatsun, Ras would have more to what he'd planned than she had known, but what purpose would visiting him serve? She'd beaten him and no longer needed his help with understanding the game. Now he might have gone with Jhon, or with others she suspected had another agenda.

Guya nodded. "It's your ship, I'm just the captain," he said. It was the same thing he'd said to her several times before, even when he'd suggested they go south. "I'll sail her where you ask, so long as you keep me entertained."

She laughed. "Help me load the boat?"

They worked quickly, carrying meat and supplies from the empty village and loading them onto the dinghy. Neither of them spoke as they worked, both seeming to know what the other needed. In much the same way, Guya seemed to know where she would go next. She appreciated that about him.

When the boat was laden with foodstuffs and other tradable items, they rowed it out into the bay, both pulling on the oars. Carth added the shadows to it, and they reached the *Goth Spald*, where Guya hurried up the ladder for her to start handing things to him.

Dara came out and watched, staring at them wordlessly. She was a shorter woman with raven black hair now pulled back into a tail tied with a deep blue sash, the marker of something from her past that Carth hadn't discovered yet. Dara carried a long-bladed knife and held it unsheathed, and with Carth instructing her, and Guya working with her, Dara had become increasingly skilled with the blade. When her gaze flicked to the village, Carth worried that she might say something, but she never did, instead turning back to the stairs leading down into the ship.

When they had unloaded, Guya looked over to Carth. "That girl… she's still not better, is she?"

"They used her, Guya. I don't know that she'll ever be 'better.'"

Guya only sighed. "You could work with her—"

"I'm not sure she's ready for me to work with her."

Guya watched the ship, noting where Dara had disappeared. "At least talk to her."

Carth sighed, nodding.

"Good. First, help me get the lines drawn and then go talk to her."

Together the two of them pulled the anchor and then they worked to get the sails unfurled. Guya moved to the helm and left Carth.

She stood in the bow, watching the sea as it parted in front of them. She could have gone to the stern and watched the village, but there was nothing for her there. The village would fade into nothingness and be forgotten, just like so many other things.

With a sigh, she turned away and headed down the stairs.

She found Dara leaning in front of a Tsatsun board, her eyes fixed on the pieces as she tried to play it by herself, reminding Carth of how she had learned to play Tsatsun while working with Ras.

Seeing her playing with the board they'd acquired months ago, Carth realized that Guya was right. She had to work with Dara, help her. Maybe she'd help herself in that way.

She pulled a chair over to the board, and Dara looked up.

"Would you like a partner?" Carth said.

The dark-haired woman smiled and nodded.

CHAPTER 2

"I STILL DON'T SEE HOW YOU MANAGED THAT MOVE," Dara said.

The stone, the piece that served as the winning move when pushed into the opponent's side of the board, rested on its side. This was a quality board that had been well carved from a speckled marble. The game board had the same black, red, and white checks of the board that she'd learned on with Ras.

Dara only had a few of Carth's pieces, and not enough to have made the game competitive. Carth had been pleased to learn that Dara knew how to play but wished she were more skilled than she was. Then again, hadn't Carth been a poor player when she'd first learned? Learning the basics and knowing how to play competitively were different matters.

"It takes practice," Carth said.

"I *have* been practicing."

She ran a hand through her raven colored hair. In the

time that Dara had traveled with them, she'd become healthier, but her eyes carried something of a haunted expression, one that deepened when they sat in the darkened room. Her skin cast a soft white glow, and Carth knew she constantly drew upon her Lashasn magic, a power they called the S'al. The same heat burned within Carth, only perhaps not quite as powerfully as it did within Dara.

"It takes time," Carth repeated.

"How long did it take for you to master it?"

Carth huffed. "I'm not certain I would claim mastery."

"I would." Dara met Carth's gaze. "How do you do it?"

Carth studied the board, thinking through what she'd learned when Ras had first begun teaching her. "You have to start thinking ahead, planning out your moves before you make them. When you believe you're thinking far enough out, then you have to start thinking of another five moves. Then five more. Eventually, you'll begin to see the moves before they're made and the game becomes easier."

"That's all you do?"

"Not all, but it's a start."

Dara placed the pieces back upright, resetting the board. "What else do you do? I want to get better. I know that's how I'm going to understand the game better than I do now, and it's how I'm going to be able to find a way to use the S'al better than I can now."

Carth smiled. "You use it well now."

"I can do better."

"We can always do better," Carth said.

Dara stared at her, the hollows of her eyes seeming caught in the shadows. "Please."

Carth sighed. She'd spoken to Ras about how she played Tsatsun, but it hadn't really made sense to her at the time how she'd been able to beat him by playing as all the people she knew. Now she understood that wasn't the way she'd beaten him, but it had given her an insight she hadn't had otherwise. That was the key, the insight to know how another might play, so that she might know what moves to make next. Eventually, she had been able to use that to see how Ras might react, and know how to beat him.

It was the same with Dara, only on a much simpler level. Tsatsun had thousands of possible moves, and Dara took many of the most obvious, the easiest, which was more a sign of her mindset than anything else. Not that she was simpleminded, but that she hadn't grasped more complex concepts. When she did, adding that to her innate empathy, Carth suspected that she would actually be formidable. For now, she was easy to defeat.

"You have to place yourself in the position of the other person," Carth said.

"Like when I play both sides of the board? I've seen you doing that, which was why I thought to try it, but I never manage to do anything other than make a few moves differently than I otherwise would have."

"It's like that, but there's something else to it as well. You have to think through what you know, and use that knowledge to play as the other person. When I first played by myself, I played as people I know, like my father and mother, building up until I was able to play with increasing complexity."

"So you play as me to defeat me?"

Carth shook her head. "I don't think that would work. When I played myself as me, I never managed to beat me. I knew what I would do, and it was easy enough to start thinking about how to counter it, even if I took a different tack. The more I played like this, the more I started mixing styles."

"Is that what you do now? You're mixing styles?"

Carth shrugged. She wasn't sure if that was how she played. Was it a mixture of styles, or was that now her? Was *her* style a combination of others'?

"I don't know."

"It works."

She nodded. "It works. Maybe it won't always. It's helpful to get a sense of how someone thinks. That's why Ras liked the game."

Dara smiled. When she did, the hollows of her eyes faded and she appeared actually happy. "What does playing this teach you about me?"

Carth shook her head. "That's not why I was playing you. I want to help you get better."

"But you come up with a judgment when you play me."

"With Tsatsun, it would be hard not to. You can learn about someone by playing them, and can come to understand them." Especially her enemies. If she could understand the Hjan—if she could know how they would react and how they would move—she would be better equipped to block them.

"And?"

Carth sighed, picking up the stone. "I can tell you're hesitant. You have some skill, but you don't have the experience using it. Other than your capture, you haven't seen hardship to push you."

Dara sat back, resting her hands in her lap. "You get all of that by playing me?"

"I get lots of things by playing you. Even if I didn't want to, I have to put myself into your perspective as we play so I can understand where you're going to move and how you're going to play out your side. The more we play—"

"I'm easy to defeat," she said, lips pressed in a pout.

"Not easy, but you haven't learned a sophisticated game."

Dara nodded. "My father taught me. He was the one gifted with the S'al. He knew how to play the game, and he was the best player in our village. Those strongest with the S'al often are the strongest players."

"I would like to have a chance to play him."

Dara shook her head. "I think you would have beat him quickly. Father… Father liked being the one everyone looked up to. I think losing to someone so young as you would have been hard on him."

"Still."

Dara swallowed and nodded.

Carth smiled. "You haven't asked to return home yet."

"I'm not ready yet."

"Why?"

Dara sighed. "I'm different than you, Carth. Not as strong. I know you want to find your father to demand he tell you why he abandoned you." Seeing Carth's face, she flushed. "I hear you with Guya. I know that's what you're after, even if you've never said it. We're searching for the Reshian. You don't have to worry that I'll do something stupid if we find them."

"I'm not worried about that," Carth said softly.

"Then why haven't you told me?"

Carth sighed. "I don't know why I'm searching for them. Or *if* I'm searching for them." That was the greater issue. She hadn't decided whether she wanted to find him again. What would she say to him? What would she expect when she found him? "My father is with them, but more than that… I don't really know. If I find him and manage to ask the questions I've had since I lost him, I don't know what I expect." She stared at the empty Tsatsun board and looked at the stone standing alone in the middle of the board. "I don't intend to demand answers from him either. I don't know what I think I'll get."

"Weren't you heading toward the Reshian when you were stranded in Odian?"

She nodded. "That had been the plan. When I left Nyaesh, they were going to bring me to the Reshian so I could learn more about my shadow abilities."

"I'd say you know how to use them well enough."

Carth frowned. "That's just it. I don' know if I do know how to use them well, or if there are things others who use the shadows could teach me. It was the same reason my mother wanted me to go to Nyaesh. She thought I might be able to use the S'al."

Dara's face lit up when she said it. "Would they teach me?"

"You'd have to become A'ras, but there's no reason they wouldn't. You have everything they want. Strength and a deep ability with what they call the A'ras flame. You might be older than they prefer, but I think they'd teach you. Invar would, at least."

"I'd love to know more. Father taught me what he could, but…"

Carth stood. What Dara asked required Carth to return to Nyaesh, and she wasn't ready for that. Carth wasn't certain she could *ever* be ready. When she'd left the last time… she had been forced away, treated like she was a traitor to the A'ras.

"We're sailing north to Lonsyn," Carth said hurriedly. "It will take a few days, but we'll get more supplies there."

Dara nodded. Carth was thankful that she didn't seem to catch how her comment had unsettled her. It shouldn't, but hearing that Dara's father had worked with her—that he had taught her—bothered her. Her own father had played games with her, but none had really prepared her for what she had faced.

Taking the Tsatsun board, she left Dara's room and stopped in the one she'd claimed for herself. She set the board down and set up the pieces. As she began the game, she played it out as Dara. As much as she wanted to help her, would she ever be able to get her to the point where she would be able to learn what she needed?

Guya thought working with Carth might help bring Dara out of her shell, but Carth didn't know if that was true or not. Since getting used by the Hjan, she'd been reserved, and the edge that Carth had first seen in her was no longer present. It might be better to bring her back to her home and let her father continue to work with her. Carth began to doubt whether she could.

———

They sailed along the outer shores, moving quickly along the coast. Standing in the peak of the bow or, occasionally, the crow's nest, gave Carth a different point of view than she had ever had before. Guya made a point of staying close to the shore, letting them see the outline of the rocks as they passed through. Dara came to the surface from time to time, but most of the time she remained belowdecks. It was as if she had no interest in seeing the landscape around them.

These were lands Carth had traveled when she was younger, but she had always done so on foot. She had not spent any time viewing them from a distance, noting the loveliness of the rock, the way it swept away from the shore and up towards the gentle sloping peak of a mountain Guya had named but Carth had already forgotten. On the third day of sailing past the village, they came across a forest that ran nearly all the way to the sea. Carth pointed and Guya nodded.

"That's the Rastor Forest," he said. "Loggers once tried to make a living cutting down trees through the forest, but they were chased away by the men who live within its borders."

Carth smiled. "There are men inside the forest who would chase away loggers?"

"Think of what you did in Nyaesh when the Hjan came. Didn't you attempt to chase them away?"

The smile faded from her face as she realized that it would've been the same. She could almost imagine living in the forest, living with the trees. There was darkness, and she would've felt welcomed there, but there was a foreboding sense within the forest as well. It reminded her that she was not alone in having magical powers; the forest itself seemed to possess a power and might of its own. Carth could almost imagine the forest attempting to keep her out, forcing her from its borders, wanting nothing to do with her shadow magic or the power of the flame.

Perhaps the S'al more than anything. What was the S'al to the forest but destruction?

They stopped on the fifth day at another village along the coast. She and Guya rowed in and then back out after finding the village empty, much like the last. Neither Carth nor Guya could speak, not knowing what to make of the emptiness within the village.

When they had nearly reached the ship, Carth sighed. "That's the second empty village. How many more will we find?"

"The second village, but I saw no sign of struggle. No sign of violence. It's as if the people within the village simply left."

Carth thought the same. At the first village, they had seen blood and what they'd thought was evidence of a struggle, but perhaps that had been wrong. What would make the villagers simply leave? What would drive people from their homes?

Playing it out, she could think of several possibilities. Violence would. She had seen it. Her father and mother had left Ih-lash because of violence in her homeland. Had the war between the A'ras and the Reshian stretched so far as to reach the coast? Who would tell the villagers the war was over, that accords were signed and peace now settled on the land?

Or was it something else? There were other things that might drive people to abandon their homes. The scarcity of resources would do so. Maybe the fishing had dried up or trade no longer came.

"Guya, did you ever trade along the coast here?"

Guya shook his head. "Hard to make it worthwhile trading in places like this. You have to anchor too deep into the sea and row yourself in. There's only so many supplies you can bring on a dinghy like this."

Carth looked at the items they had brought from the village. Most were simple foodstuffs. "You'd bring your supplies to Lonsyn, and then what would happen?"

"In Lonsyn, the merchants would request various items, picking and choosing from what came in off the ships and what they would know would sell. They'd take these down the coast, I presume. There is only so much trade that can happen in a place like Lonsyn, and the merchants wouldn't see the same value to collecting goods as they would outside of the city."

Once back about the ship, they secured the dinghy. Dara didn't question what had happened. She was observant, and Carth suspected she knew that something had come to the village. They passed several more villages much the same on their way to Lonsyn. With each one, Carth struggled with why. Why were villages so close to Lonsyn empty?

Carth had been resting in her bunk when a knock came at her door. She was in the middle of a game, playing as Ras again and trying to get him to beat her when she played as herself, but he could not.

Dara glanced at the board when she opened the door, her face ashen.

"What is it?"

"You have to come," she said.

Carth made another move and then followed Dara.

CHAPTER 3

THE SUN CAST STRANGE SHADOWS WHEN CARTH REACHED the deck of the ship, and she grasped for them without waiting for what she might find. Whatever had happened here had been upsetting to Dara. Considering all they had been through together, anything that could upset Dara that much must be truly awful.

Guya stood at the railing near the bow, staring down toward the sea. Carth slid toward him, gliding on the shadows.

When she reached him, she noted the stench in the air. It started gradually and built quickly. The stink was that of rot, like an animal sitting in the sun, or fish washed up on the shore, or… a body lying with its throat slit in a dinghy.

Gulls had pecked at the body, leaving chunks of flesh missing from its cheeks. Where the eyes had been, there were now hollows, nothing more than bloody gaping wounds. Even the ears were missing. Bits of cloth had been torn free as well, though it was clear that the person had once been dressed in a long dark cloak. Black hair was matted with blood.

"Where did they come from?" Carth asked.

Guya glanced over, and she noted the color had drained from his face. He'd seen as much as she had over the last few months, and this had challenged him in a way that little else had. "Just saw it floating here."

"And where is here?" Carth surveyed the horizon but didn't see any land nearby.

"Middle of the Great-Watcher-be-damned ocean. There's nothing else around us, and certainly no reason a little clap of a boat like that should be out here on its own."

"You ever see anything like that?" Dara asked.

Carth shouldn't be surprised that Dara held herself together as well as she did. She had proven herself stronger than Carth would have suspected the first time they had met. Maybe her abduction had made her stronger than Carth had realized, or maybe she only pretended to hold it together. Given what she'd seen from Dara recently, the quiet and the hesitation, that was more likely.

"Unfortunately, I have," Guya said.

Carth turned to him. "You have?"

"It's considered a sign of disrespect. Leave a man to die in the midst of the sea, no oars, nothing but the sun and the salt water for company. Most kill themselves like this one here."

Carth frowned, studying the body. Through the blood and the bits of flesh, she could make out few details about it, but enough to tell her that something wasn't quite as it appeared. "There's a couple of problems with that, Guya." When he turned to her, she went on. "First, that's a woman. Second, where's the knife?"

Guya blinked, the puzzlement that flittered across his face fading quickly. "Well, damn," he whistled. "Even worse that it happened to some poor lass."

Carth laughed bitterly. "Some poor lass? Are you sure about that? That could have been me. Would you have called me a poor lass?"

He shrugged. "Might be I would. You've got gentle enough features. Then I get to know you and I'd wonder if you deserved it."

Carth frowned. "What do you think happened here?"

"There would have been someone who came through here and left them. We'll probably never know why or when."

Carth pulled on the shadows, drawing the small vessel toward her, and jumped down to the dinghy.

Inside the small boat, the stench was even more pronounced. She held her nose, trying to ignore the stink, but gagged regardless. Up close, the body's decay was easier to see. The hunks of flesh missing made the body more grotesque. Blood had clotted in some places, but not completely.

How was that possible?

Carth touched the blood. It was still wet.

A pool of it had accumulated in the bottom of the boat. This was congealed, a layer of thick and deep maroon forming a strange shape. The death was fresh enough that there should be other signs of what happened here.

She looked up toward Dara and Guya. Both stood at the railing, neither saying anything. Like Guya had said, leaving the body floating like this seemed like an insult of some kind. A message. What could this woman have done to deserve this?

Nothing.

No one deserved this.

There wasn't anything on the body that would explain what happened here. After all the time she'd spent chasing down the Hjan, it was almost a relief to find something without any magical cause.

Pulling on the ring she wore on her middle finger, she sent a surge of S'al magic, that which she'd once called the A'ras flame, through her and into the bow of the dinghy. Fire licked at the wood, gradually taking hold.

Releasing the S'al, she drew upon the strength of the shadows and launched herself back onto the deck of the *Goth Spald*. She scanned the horizon, noting darkness moving in the distance. Carth tried shifting the shadows, cloaking herself briefly. Doing so could often allow her to see more clearly, but it didn't help her this time. Darkness meant clouds, land, or other ships. They weren't near land, and the sky was mostly clear. That left only one other possibility.

Tearing her gaze from the distance, she turned to Guya. The captain stood with his muscled arms crossed over his thick chest. The way his brow furrowed, the deep sun-kissed wrinkles creating shadows of their own, told her all she needed to know about his feelings about what they'd seen.

"I couldn't leave her like that," she said to Guya.

"Wouldn't have expected it of you."

Carth gazed into the boat. The flames had spread, leaping from the bow and reaching the dead woman. When they touched the blood, it crackled softly. Carth almost imagined sparks of flame within it.

"We should keep going," she said to Guya. She used a hint of shadow magic to push their ship forward. "You don't want to risk the flames spreading to the *Spald*."

"Thought you could control them if they did."

The fire had consumed the small vessel, now situated behind the stern of the boat. At the pace they were sailing —and with the addition of her power—they would move well beyond it quickly. The flames were bright, and getting brighter, and she could still feel the heat coming off of it, though wasn't sure if that was something she imagined through her connection to the S'al or whether it was real.

"I can, but we still need to be careful. And that's not why we're going to want to get going."

Dara looked up. She'd been staring into the water, following the burning dinghy as they passed, her eyes seeing something that Carth couldn't quite make out.

Carth pointed into the distance. "There's ships moving out there. I can't tell how many, but with flames like that…"

Dara's eyes widened slightly.

Guya nodded and relaxed. "Nothing is going to catch the *Goth Spald*," he told Dara. "Don't hurt to get tacking a little more easterly, though."

He hurried off, leaving Dara and Carth standing at the bow. Spray would hit Carth in the face, and she'd wipe it off, only to have more strike her. It left her dark hair constantly damp, and with the cool breeze, slightly chilled. That was probably the reason Dara held on to the power of the S'al, giving her skin a soft glow. Carth had seen how powerful she could be with it, strong enough that the Hjan had intended to use her against the Reshian.

"You've seen this before," Carth said to her.

Dara blinked slowly and nodded.

"What is it?"

Dara licked her lips, taking a deep breath, finally managing to tear her gaze from the water and the now-distant fire. "When they came for me," she started, a hitch clear in her voice, "we knew enough to hide. It wasn't the first time slavers had come toward Ganduhl, and I doubted it will be the last."

"They wanted your abilities, or those like you."

"That time," Dara agreed. "There were other times when men would come, always on fast ships, carrying swords or crossbows or…" She shook her head. "They would take girls. Sometimes only one or two. Others times, they would take as many as they could carry. My father… my father fought, but that day the S'al wasn't strong within him."

Dara fell silent as she squeezed the railing in a white-knuckled grip. The ship groaned as it moved through the waves, with the wind snapping the sails.

Finally, she looked up again. "When the villages resisted, they would take a woman. Not a girl, not like they preferred, but a woman. If we were lucky, she'd float back to shore a few days later, but we weren't lucky often."

Carth looked back toward the dinghy. The flames had subsided somewhat, but the dark shapes on the horizon grew larger. There were at least three ships, all with massive square sails, heading in their direction. Guya was right about the *Spald* in that it was fast, but they weren't racing away from those ships. If they were unlucky, they'd get cut off.

"They were like that?" Carth asked.

"Like that. Sometimes worse. Throats were always slit, and the bodies were often chewed at by the birds, but they came back. It gave us a certain sense of closure, and for that we felt a twisted sense of thanks."

Carth shook her head. Things like that happening bothered her. They were things she couldn't stop, that she couldn't change, even if she wanted to. How could she intervene when slavers attacked small villages?

"I'm sorry," she said. There was nothing else for her to say, nothing she could tell Dara that would make the horrors that some of the island villagers experienced any better. There was nothing she could say that would change things.

She had brought peace to a people, but she still felt powerless in some ways.

"That's why I'm with you. If there's anything I can learn, anything I can do that will help prevent others from going through that, I want to do it."

When Dara started sobbing, Carth pulled her into a close embrace and hugged her, letting the emotion wash over her. Dara sagged into her, sobbing heavily for long moments before finally taking a deep breath and stepping back.

"I'm… I'm fine."

"I know. And I'll make sure you learn what you need to know to keep yourself safe."

"That's just it, Carth. I don't want to keep only myself safe. I want to learn whatever I can to keep those I care about safe too. I want to be able to return home and make certain that no one else suffers the way those in my village did."

Carth started to tell her she would see to it that Dara learned to use her ability with the S'al well enough that no one would be able to attack her people, and that she would help ensure that it didn't continue to happen, but there wasn't a way for her to ensure it didn't happen.

But maybe there could be.

Now that she'd created a sort of peace—tenuous though it might be—she needed to make certain that others didn't suffer. Wasn't that the best way for her to use her abilities?

So far it was her, Dara with Guya, but that didn't mean they couldn't collect additional help.

They'd been sailing for weeks. Weeks upon weeks. And during that time, Carth hadn't decided what she wanted to do, other than her vague assertions that she eventually wanted to find the Reshian and understand her shadow abilities. Guya had given her space and had been willing to sail her wherever she asked, but it was time for her to decide on a different plan.

Which meant recruiting others to help.

But help with what?

She looked at Dara, thinking about the group of women who had been trapped on the ship with her, women who had been taken from their homes, but who had been helpless. With Carth's ability with the shadows, and with the S'al, it was possible for her to prevent others from suffering as well. All she had to do was decide, but it was a decision she so far hadn't been willing to make. Carth still wasn't sure if she was ready, but she thought she had to be. If she didn't do it, who would?

"We've got a stop in Lonsyn," she said to Dara, "and then we'll make our way to Nyaesh." She stared at the ships and noted that Guya had put distance between them. They would move beyond those ships now.

"Why?"

"Because you need training if you're going to get strong enough that others can't hurt you. There's only so much I can teach."

The muscles in Dara's jaw clenched as she nodded.

Carth wasn't sure what sort of welcome she'd receive in Nyaesh. Now that they had peace with the Reshian, it couldn't be what it once would have been. But knowing that didn't change the nausea that gnawed at the pit of her stomach.

CHAPTER 4

A SOMBER AIR OVERTOOK THEM AS THEY SAILED. CARTH played Tsatsun, preferring to play by herself. Occasionally she would play with Dara, though Dara didn't progress very fast. Had it been the same with Ras? Had that been the reason he'd preferred to play Tsatsun alone more often than not? Dara was descended from Lashasn. At least while playing, Dara slowly managed to emerge from her shell, and she began to demonstrate some of the humor Carth remembered from when she'd first met her.

Shouldn't Dara have *more* skill than she did? Carth tried not to let it trouble her when they played, and tried not to take it out on Dara, but Dara didn't seem to notice any subtleties about the game.

Guya sailed with a determination he hadn't shown before. Carth wasn't certain whether it came from the fact that they had a destination once they reached Lonsyn, or whether he worried that she'd change her mind. He remained mostly silent.

The third day after finding the remains of the woman, Carth spied another ship in the distance.

It headed in much the same direction, sailing along the coast as if making its way toward Lonsyn. When she pointed it out to Guya, he studied it through his spyglass.

"That's a fast ship, Carth. Doubt we'll overtake her."

She borrowed the glass from him and stared at the ship through it. It had a sleek and narrow hull and massive wide sails. It *should* streak through the water, but it didn't appear to be moving nearly as fast as she would have expected.

"It's slowing," she noted.

Guya grabbed the glass and whistled softly as he did. "Damn, but you be right. I can tack us around so we don't get too close—"

Carth shook her head. "Don't."

"We don't want to run afoul of another ship like that on open water. There's only the three of us."

She grinned at him. "Are you really worried about what might happen if we come across another ship?"

He nodded. "You have to be, Carth. There are dangerous men out on the seas, men who want nothing but to hurt the next ship and take what they can. Think of what you saw back in that village. For that matter, think about what you saw when we found her." He motioned to Dara. "Too many only look for what they can take."

"I am thinking of that."

Guya's eyes widened and he scratched his chin. It had been several days since he'd shaved, and the black-and-gray-peppered growth was getting long for him. "She'd be swift enough for what we saw, wouldn't she?"

"Not much storage," Carth said.

"Don't need much if you're only moving people."

"You seem to know a bit about slaving."

His brow furrowed. "You don't get out on the sea if you're a fool. I've seen enough to know what men think they can get away with. There's not much of a market for slaves in the north, but to the south…"

"What about the south?" All that Carth had heard about was the Hjan. There would be other problems in the south, but they weren't hers.

"There are places where these women have value. They train them, keep them as courtesans."

"Courtesans?"

"Whores. Women the men will use for their own purposes, things like—"

"You've made your point," Carth said. Her mind started puzzling through what Guya said, but it didn't entirely make sense to her. "Why take them from here and move them south? That seems like an awful lot of work. Wouldn't it be cheaper and easier to bring women from the south to these places?"

"You'd think so, but they don't work quite like that. Prefer to keep them scared. They don't want these women knowing they have a chance of escape. You get them into a foreign city and with none they know, some who don't even speak the language, and what choice do they have?"

"There's always a choice."

Guya grunted. "The choice is death. That's not much of a choice if you ask me."

They drew closer to the narrow-bodied ship. As they

did, Dara stood, finally noting the other ship, her eyes widening. "What are we doing so close to them?"

Guya pointed to Carth. "This one thinks to get us closer to it. I suspect she intends to board."

Carth flashed a hard smile. "I thought about it."

"How close do you need for me to be?"

Carth looked up at the sun. At this time of day, the sun was bright and burned off most of the shadows. There were always some coming off the sails, but they were faint, and not enough to be of much use to her. The power of the S'al would work, but then she didn't have the same control over it as she did the shadows.

"Close," she said.

Guya remained at the helm. When Carth glanced over to him, she noted the way his knuckles whitened around the wheel, matching the clench to his jaw. His dark eyes were narrowed to slits.

Carth moved to the railing and Dara followed. "You should go below," she suggested to Dara.

"If you're going to risk yourself and go aboard, I'm going with you."

Carth shot her a look. "This isn't the time for you to make a stand. Go below. I'll take care of this."

"What if they have some way of stopping you?"

Carth doubted they would. If they were slavers, they would be brutes, but she doubted they were powered in any way. She unsheathed her knives, gripping them tightly. "I have other abilities as well."

She climbed to the top of the railing, balancing on it as they neared the other ship. They were close enough now that she could make out three men wearing nothing but breeches on the other deck. Two of them held crossbows, aimed at her.

Carth smiled.

There was a part of her that enjoyed the fight. That part of her welcomed the violence, and welcomed the danger. If these men were a part of the attacks on the women, she would do what was needed.

She leaped.

As she did, she exploded the S'al through her, using that power to propel her across the water and carry her toward the distant ship. She'd used shadows this way before but had never used the S'al to power her crossing like this.

One of the men fired his crossbow at her while she sailed toward him.

Carth tumbled in the air and came rolling onto the deck.

Knives flashed as she did, and she pressed out in a heat ring from her, mixing with the shadows that coalesced around the ship. Carth drew on this, hiding within the shadows as she pierced the two men's shoulders with crossbow bolts. They didn't need to die, and this way she could ask questions of them.

The last man had a sword, but she was quicker than him. She caught him along his wrist, and he dropped the sword, which clattered to the deck of the ship.

She kicked, dropping the first man, and swept her leg around, catching the other crossbowman. The man with the sword backed away from her, but she didn't let him get too far and knocked him into the deck railing. Much harder and he would have gone overboard.

The *Goth Spald* pulled alongside and Guya looped ropes around the railing, crossing over and quickly beginning to tie the men up.

"What do you intend to do with them?" he asked as he bound the first of the men with thick rope.

Carth released her connection to the shadows but maintained the connection to the flame, letting it burn through her softly. When she did, the other sailors looked at her, eyes wide.

"Reshian," the largest of them said. He had been the man with the sword. His eyes were a pale green and he was tall and solidly built, if not quite as powerfully built as Guya.

"Not Reshian," Guya said, pushing him back against the railing.

"She used the shadows. I saw it. Only the Reshian can do that."

While Guya worked on securing the other two men, Carth crouched in front of the man she presumed to be the captain. "What do you have on board?"

"Supplies I'm bringing to Lonsyn."

She sniffed. "Supplies. Like the kind of supplies you took from the village three days south?"

The twitch at the corner of his eyes was enough confirmation for her.

"What did you do to them?"

The man shook his head. "It wasn't me. I'm not a slaver."

Carth considered striking him, but refrained. It might make her feel better, but that wasn't going to get her any answers.

Keeping her knives ready, she made her way below. Down here, without any lighting, the shadows were thicker and she felt better connected to them. She maintained that connection, holding on to it so that she could see through the dimness of the shadows.

The storage area was different than Guya's ship. Whereas the *Goth Spald* had three doors, a separate quarters behind each, with a holding area for cargo, this ship had a single door. Carth opened it carefully, not certain what she might find.

On the other side of the door, faint light filtered through the portholes. Two rows of bunks lined the wall. A table rested in the middle. Against the opposite wall were casks that reminded her of the ale Guya intended to transport from Asador. Talun had used the casks to hide the girls stolen from Odian.

She popped one of the casks open and found it filled with grain. The next held a watery wine. The next contained ale. Carth stopped before opening each of them.

They were as the men had claimed.

Why had they slowed?

She had assumed they had been slavers, especially after what she'd seen from the village and the woman in the boat, but that hadn't been the case at all.

Traders, at least as far as she could tell.

Carth made a quick circle through the hold but didn't find anything else.

She'd made a mistake.

It wasn't the first time, and her mind worked through how to make reparations as she climbed the stairs back to the deck. When she reached the top, the first thing that caught her eyes was the pool of blood near where Guya had been holding the prisoners.

"Guya?" she asked.

He grunted, "Stop!"

She raced toward him, ripping the power of the flame through her, letting it burn. Had she more connection to the shadows, she would have used them as well.

In spite of all the blood, he was unharmed.

Dara stood next to Guya, and she clutched the captain's long sword between both hands. Carth had been working with her to master using knives, but they hadn't spent much time with the sword. Blood coated the blade, leaving droplets across the deck between her and the captain, who now sagged forward, his belly split open. One of the other sailors also lay dead, cut much like the captain.

Carth realized Guya blocked her from reaching the third man.

The other sailor was bound and tried crawling away from Dara, his eyes fixed on her. Guya held his hands out as if he intended to stop her weaponless.

Carth flickered forward, using a combination of the faint shadows she could find on the ship and the power of the flame burning through her, and caught Dara on the wrists, knocking the sword from her hands.

"What happened?" Carth said, turning to Guya.

The captain nodded toward Dara. "She came aboard, grabbed that sword, and started cutting. Then you came up. You know about as much as me."

"Dara?" she asked.

Dara blinked. "They were taking slaves," she said. "Like the ship that took me and the others. My sister." She licked her lips, her eyes still wide. "Like what happened to that village. I saw how you returned with everything you brought to trade. I don't need you to tell me what that means, just like I don't need to see that woman you burned on the boat to know they killed her too. They need to suffer for what they did."

"They don't have slaves," Carth said.

Guya tipped his head and frowned, but said nothing.

Dara blinked slowly as the comment sank in. "No slaves?"

Carth shook her head. "They're traders, just like they said they were."

"Traders?"

"Go below. See for yourself."

Dara made her way below, leaving Carth and Guya alone with the remaining sailor. Carth noted the sounds of Dara's footsteps on the boards, mixing with the groaning of the ship.

"I can't believe she'd do this," Carth said, looking at the pool of blood. The air stank of blood and the foul odor of spilled entrails.

"She snapped, Carth. Happens on the sea."

Carth should have worked with Dara more closely. She might have realized what was happening if she had, and she might have been able to head some of it off. She'd told her to go belowdecks and hadn't expected Dara to attack the way that she had. For that matter, she hadn't expected Dara to come aboard the ship in the first place.

"There was no sign of slavers?" Guya asked.

She shook her head. "Grain. Ale. Some wine. We'll need to bring it aboard, along with him," she said, motioning to the remaining sailor.

"What do you intend to do with him?"

She grunted. "What we should have done with the others. Let him go. We'll get him to Lonsyn, or near enough, and free him."

"And the ship?"

Carth debated what to do with the other ship. Without a captain and a crew, it made more sense to burn it like she had the dinghy, but she couldn't bring herself to do it.

"I'll beach it and row back out to you."

"You don't have to do it yourself."

She looked over to the *Goth Spald*. "I think I do. You need to watch Dara and keep her from him," she said, motioning toward their prisoner.

"You could leave him on shore, too."

That might be better, she realized. Bringing him into Lonsyn would only open them up to questions, especially if she intended to release him. They could leave him belowdecks until they did, but she didn't want to risk him getting free and setting others after them.

"That might be best," she agreed.

Dara clomped up the stairs, her eyes slightly wide. She said nothing as she reached the railing and climbed back over to the *Goth Spald*. Guya followed, leaving Carth with the ship.

The time she'd spent with Guya had trained her to handle it alone reasonably well. The sailor watched her as she took the wheel and started toward the shore. Guya followed close enough, but he wouldn't come all the way into shore.

"What's the ship's name?" Carth asked when the rocky shore came into view.

The sailor said nothing.

"If you want me to free you, tell me what the ship's name is."

"*Tempar.*"

The word carried something of old Ih to it, but Carth didn't know the language well enough to recognize it. The man watched her as she turned the wheel, bringing them closer and closer toward the shore.

"Where were you headed?" Carth asked, wanting only to break the silence between them while they sailed.

"Lonsyn. Same as you, I imagine."

"Why did you slow and wait for us, then?"

The man didn't answer.

Carth turned her attention to him from the wheel. "I know you were slowing. I saw it. So tell me why."

"We thought you might be someone else."

"What else?"

He shook his head.

There was no reason for him to be secretive, especially as she had essentially promised him that she would release him. If he went quiet, he risked his freedom more than if he shared.

She thought about the supplies in the casks. They were for trade, and there was nothing particularly impressive about them. They might get them some traction, but in Lonsyn?

None of that explained why the ship had slowed when

encountering another… unless they were expecting a *different* ship.

Carth looked up, scanning the horizon.

There was nothing.

She released the wheel and jumped from the *Tempar* back to the *Goth Spald*. Guya grunted in surprise when she reached him. "They were waiting for another ship," Carth said.

"Another? No reason to meet on the seas unless… oh."

Carth nodded. "That's my concern too."

"Maybe Dara was right to take them out."

"Maybe. Are you interested in helping with this?" she asked.

Guya let out a deep sigh. "What do you have in mind?"

"I think we need to see what they were going to do." He frowned. "It's time for us to get a little information."

"How do you propose we do that?"

She shrugged. "We'll have to be someone else. We're going to be the *Tempar*."

CHAPTER 5

Guya anchored up the coast, leaving Dara in control of the *Goth Spald*. There was a part of Carth that worried what Dara might do, or what might happen if one of the ships they intended to meet came across her, but she didn't want Dara involved in this, not until she knew how she would react. It wasn't easy to know *how* she might react. A few days ago, she would have expected Dara to have been reserved, but she no longer thought that would happen with her.

They sailed on the *Tempar*, cruising along the coast but not moving with any real speed. Speed would have prevented them from detecting the other ship they intended to intercept, and they needed to be ready for it.

"I don't see anything," Guya said, holding the spyglass to his eye.

Carth didn't either, though she used a different technique, twisting the shadows around the late afternoon so that she could clear the darkness. It was a trick only, one that gave her a slightly heightened sense of what might be cruising on the sea, but still a trick. There had to be a better way.

"He claims they were meeting someone around here." She motioned to the man lying bound to the mast. He stared at them but hadn't said anything more. Carth suspected he hadn't believed she would have risked herself on this meeting.

"Lonsyn isn't far. They could have sailed on…"

That was a possibility, and as she played out that in her mind, she realized that it was more likely. If the other ship had come through and not found who they expected, they would likely have continued sailing on to the next port. There was no other option beyond here other than Lonsyn, not unless they wanted to cross the sea.

"We'll keep a watch," she said.

Carth made her way to the captive and crouched in front of him. She'd found holding one of her knives had the effect of drawing his attention, and made a point of running the flat of her blade across the back of her arm. If it intimidated him somewhat, it would be worth it.

"When were you to meet?" she asked again.

He stared at her with a baleful gaze. "Kill me or leave me, Reshian."

It was the first time he'd spoken in several hours. Carth considered that a slight victory. "I've told you, I'm not Reshian."

He sniffed. "You use the shadows like the Reshian."

"And I use the flame like the A'ras," she said, pointing her knife toward her and drawing power through her mother's ring as she pressed outward. Heat built, nothing but the slightest amount, just enough for him to know that she *could* push on it. She wrapped it around him, not with the same subtlety or strength as someone like Invar would have managed, but more than she ever would have done prior to discovering the way she could use her mother's ring.

His eyes widened slightly. "A'ras. They wouldn't let you leave."

"They didn't want me." She slipped her knife back into the sheath at her waist. "Now. When were you meeting them?"

His gaze shifted. It was brief, barely more than a flicker, but she saw the way his focus turned to the setting sun.

"Dusk?"

It would be a dangerous time, but had the advantage that anyone who might get too close wouldn't see what they were doing. A perfect time for slaving.

"Kill me or—"

She struck him on the side of his head, and he slumped over. "Release you. I know."

Carth sighed and stood, holding the handle of her knife as she stared out over the sea. She saw nothing to tell her that any other ships were out there.

Guya shook his head slightly. "We're not getting anything here. They might not even have come this way, Carth. Lonsyn wouldn't be as sympathetic to the slavers as places farther to the south."

"We'll give it a little longer," she suggested.

Guya shrugged and turned his attention back to the bow.

Carth stood at the railing, holding on to the shadows. As she did, she realized that she had been cloaking the ship, even if unintentionally. Pulling on the shadows in this way created layers of darkness around them, and there was enough growing darkness that she could pull everything around her into it.

They continued to sail and the sun began settling on the horizon, a glowing ball of orange and red filtering through the thick clouds. It was beautiful and peaceful. The sun hit the water, then disappeared, leaving only the streaks of color.

She felt pressure on the shadows.

There was no other way to describe what she detected. Something pressed upon the connection she held, as if trying to part the shadows.

If this was the other ship they expected, she didn't want to obstruct them from reaching them. Carth eased back on her connection, letting it fade away from her, disappearing slightly. She held on to it, clinging to the edge of the shadows.

Had she created a barrier of some kind?

She hadn't known the shadows could work like that. She'd seen A'ras masters use the flame in such a way, but she hadn't had the same education with the shadows. Everything she did with them she had learned on her own. Likely there were things those much more experienced using the shadows would be able to teach her, if only she could find them. That had been the purpose of sailing for the Reshian with Jhon before she'd been stranded in Odian.

"See it?" Guya asked.

He held the spyglass up to his face and stared through it, looking toward the south.

Carth took the glass from him and peered through it. At first she saw nothing, but she added the connection she had to the shadows and let them guide her. She *had* detected something on the sea, and if she could only follow where it was…

There.

A twin-masted ship with a wider hull than the one they were on parted the waves as it sailed toward them. Wide maroon sails caught the wind, reminding her in some ways of the A'ras sash they wore as markers of rank. Carth noted two people on the deck, and another hiding within the crow's nest.

"I see it. How did you see it first?"

Guya's eyes narrowed. "You sail long enough, you begin to see the way the currents work."

"Sounds like they're alive."

"In some ways, they are. The entire sea is alive, and we're just traveling on her."

"Her?"

Guya smiled. "Aye, the sea is most definitely a woman. You get too arrogant, you try to push too hard, and the sea will crush you. If you give her enough respect, she'll take you on a ride you'll never forget."

Carth shook her head. "Sailors can be disgusting."

"Some can," he agreed.

They closed in on the other ship. She maintained her connection to the flame, holding it burning deep within her. Not only to the flame, but to a trickle of shadows as well. If needed, she could surge through them.

They caught a wave, and their captive groaned.

"Damn," Guya said. "Need to get him below so they don't see we've got someone tied up."

Carth quickly cut the ropes holding the captive to the mast, leaving his wrists and ankles bound, and carried him below. She drew on her shadow magic to clear the darkness and tucked him onto one of the bunks, securing his wrists to the rail, before running back up to the surface.

The other ship was near enough that she could see the faces of the other sailors.

These were all dark-skinned people, their faces so deeply tanned and weathered as to be almost brown. They wore long pants bound at the ankles, and the two she noted on the deck wore shirts opened to reveal their chests. She flicked her gaze to the crow's nest and was surprised to note a woman there. She wore clothes much like the men's, though her shirt was tied closed.

"You're not Urnash," the nearest man said.

He had his hand on the hilt of his sword, and his brown eyes swept over the surface of the ship. Carth had scrubbed the blood from the deck as much as she could, but there was still some staining. She hoped it wasn't too obvious and that they didn't ask many questions. With the growing dark, it should pass.

"Aye, not Urnash," Guya said with a shrug. He stepped toward the rail, walking with a dangerous sort of gait. "Urnash thought he'd take our cut and split. Instead, he's the one who got split."

They hadn't discussed how they would explain the captain's absence, but Guya played it perfectly. He added the right amount of menace to his words, making it convincing. Had she not known him as she did, she would have believed that he *would* have killed Urnash.

"The deal was with Urnash."

Guya shrugged again. "Maybe. You don't want to trade, we'll take the grain and the ale on to Lonsyn."

The other man's eyes narrowed. "If you were with Urnash, you would know you came from Lonsyn. Why would you return?"

Carth could see Guya hesitate.

It was too long. The sailors pulled crossbows out and aimed them at Guya and Carth.

The ship had come from Lonsyn? She thought of the supplies, realizing that they had missed something. Where were they heading?

She looked at the railing, then out over the sea. Something was wrong.

Carth didn't know where the ship had been headed, but if it really had come from Lonsyn, this wasn't what she'd thought it was. It was worse.

She glanced to Guya, barely taking her eyes off the crossbows. "This might get ugly."

"Where you going? Don't leave me to get bolts through me."

"I won't. And you won't."

Carth jumped across the distance between the two ships. When she landed on the deck, she went rolling. The nearest sailor, one who appeared to have ink smeared on his chest, dropped his crossbow and quickly unsheathed his sword. She jumped in, pulling the shadows towards her, wrapping them around her like a cloak. Darkness settled around her. She slashed out with her knife, catching him in his stomach. She pressed the shadows out with the attack. They crawled through him, quickly darkening his skin.

The man grunted and fell forward.

Carth stood and searched the deck of the ship for the other sailors. The woman in the crow's nest had started climbing down with a crossbow in her hand. Carth leaped towards her, pressing out with the shadows and pulling on the S'al flame as well. As she did, she caught the woman's wrist with her knife and sent out the power of the flame. The woman convulsed and then stopped moving.

The remaining sailor was gone.

Carth looked around but didn't see him. She raced towards the stairs leading below decks. Everything here was dark. There was a bitter scent, that of incense or medicines burned, scents that she had smelled before, though the last time had been when she was a child working with her mother. Her mother had dabbled as an herbalist and had large collections of spices and leaves and oils, all of which she'd used for different concoctions for healing. These were used for a different purpose, one with a foul undertone.

She pulled on the shadows, removing the darkness.

Carth gasped.

Bodies were splayed around the hold. She counted nearly a dozen, all injured and bleeding. Someone whimpered in a corner, and she turned to them, but she was too late. The sailor sliced this person across the throat, spilling blood onto the floorboards of the ship.

Carth jumped towards him in anger, knives unsheathed, pressing shadows and flame through the knives. The sailor moved quickly, taking blood from the woman he had just killed and smearing it across his chest and back. Muscles rippled beneath his flesh.

He changed before her.

She had no other words that would describe what she saw. Where he had been a thinner man, ropy with muscle, now he was large, more muscular even than Guya. He grunted and leapt towards her, two swords unsheathed. He attacked with an unexpected violence.

Had she not had her training with the A'ras, she would have stood no chance. As it was, even with her training, she had only her knives, and he had a longer reach.

Carth jumped back, tripping over a dead body. She scrambled backwards and her hand slipped in a pool of blood.

"The Reshian think they can *attack* now?" There was a hint of eagerness in his voice. "We have waited for this."

"I'm not Reshian."

As she said it, Carth pulled on the shadows, wrapping them around her so that she cloaked herself, sinking into the shadows.

Pressure pushed against her cloaking. She crawled backwards, using the shadows for strength and power. To this, she added the flame magic as well.

With shadow and flame, she sent her magic coursing through her—and through the knives. It struck him in the chest, throwing him backwards. There was no need for finesse, no need for anything other than brutality. It was a good thing, as Carth was only capable of brutality. She had not mastered the subtler parts to her magic.

The man shook himself as he studied her, a dark smile playing across his face. Casually, he leaned forward and touched his hand to the pool of blood from the women he'd slaughtered, bringing his hand to his mouth before running his tongue along his palm. His eyes closed and a sick satisfied expression crossed his face.

He rippled again.

Somehow, he was drawing power from the blood of those he sacrificed. If she remained, she would be his next victim.

Carth pulled on the shadows and the flame, pressing through her mother's ring, through the knives that she carried, and sent this combined power against him.

Magic struck him and threw him backwards.

Knowing there wasn't much time, Carth searched for anyone else who might be alive, looking at the captives. None lived.

Holding on to her magic, she sank into the shadows and slid towards the stairs, climbing them quickly. At the top of the stair, she created a barrier using the flame magic that burned inside her.

Chaos greeted her on the deck of the ship.

The two people she thought she had killed both still lived and faced Guya on the *Tempar*.

She jumped, the power of her magic carrying her across the distance between the two boats, and landed on the deck with Guya.

He needed her help, but first she needed to prevent an attack by the other man.

She spun, flames pressing out from her knives, and used the S'al magic against the other ship. She had done this once before when she had rescued Dara. As they had then, the flames crept slowly. She drew more, pulling this power through her mother's ring, and felt the surge of the magic beneath her skin and within her blood. With a thunderous explosion, the ship cracked under the power of her attack.

Carth joined Guya, and the two of them faced the woman from the crow's nest and the man she thought she'd already killed. Shadows did not seem to have worked on them, almost as if they possessed some resistance to them. She noticed maroon smears upon the man's skin and clothes that she had thought ink at first. Now she understood what it was. They used some sort of blood magic to protect and strengthen them.

Shadows didn't work against it, but would the flame?

She dropped her connection to the shadow magic, and pressed power through her mother's ring. She drew this through the knife she carried, the one that Invar had given her. It surged a bright white, blindingly so, and had she not lowered her connection to the shadows, she might not have been able to reach it so directly.

Power filled her, the S'al leaving her practically glowing.

The two attackers turned their attention to her.

Filled with power as she was, they were no match for her. She stabbed the woman with her knife, cutting across her belly before remembering that had not worked the last time. Carth spun, driving her heel into the woman's forehead, and slammed her knife into her throat. The other man backed away from her and reached the railing of the ship before she could catch him. He jumped, disappearing into the water.

Carth and Guya stood at the railing, looking down at the sea, but he did not resurface. Moments passed, and they saw nothing more of him.

Finally, with a harsh crack, the other ship sank with burning anger into the depths of the ocean.

CHAPTER 6

"What happened there?"

Carth looked at Dara, wondering how much to tell the woman. Did she tell her about the way the other people had been slaughtered beneath the ship? Could she tell her about the way they had somehow used a blood magic to power themselves?

She had never seen anything like that before. There were many magics in the world, and she had seen several of them herself, but what she had experienced on that ship was horrific. The more she thought about it, the more she realized they couldn't have been dead that long before the *Tempar* had arrived, but if that was the case, they had *always* intended to kill them.

"They were gone," are said. She had washed her hands in the sea before abandoning the ship and the sailor they had tied once more to the mast. Guya had not wanted to kill him, but Carth was not willing to free him either. In many ways, leaving him like that was a worse punishment

54

than death. If he knew anything about what had happened on the other ship, he hadn't said.

"Gone?"

Carth looked at her hands, unable to meet the other woman's eyes. How could she admit what she had seen? She suspected the women on that ship were from the empty village. She suspected something worse had happened to the men.

Dara needed the truth. If she didn't have the truth, how would she be able to handle the future? Her only concern was the amount of aggression she had already seen from Dara. The woman had suffered, but had suffered at the hands of slavers. The men on that ship had been something else, something worse.

"They were dead," she whispered.

Dara looked from her to Guya and nodded. "What did you do?"

"What was needed."

Dara sighed before going back below decks, leaving Carth and Guya alone. Neither had spoken much after leaving the other ship. She wondered if Guya knew how she had ignited the *Tempar* so that it would never sail again, leaving the last sailor to die. It was a horrible fate, but she couldn't deny he deserved it. The way he looked at her left her suspecting that Guya knew.

"Have you ever seen anything like that before?" she asked.

"I have not. I have sailed these seas and never seen anything like that before."

They had turned the ship towards Lonsyn, both determined to sail through the night. Using her power over the shadows, they were able to sail safely. She added a slight push, drawing on the power she found within them, and was able to speed the ship along. Waves crashed along the side of the ship, leaving a steady creaking sound that mixed with the occasional cawing from gulls. The air had the scent of salt, but she still could not get rid of the memory of the bitter stink from below the deck of the ship, nor could she get rid of the smell of the blood, still far too fresh by the time she'd arrived.

"That kind of power will draw the Hjan," Guya said.

Carth suspected the same thing. She seemed to possess a certain resistance to the shadow magic that would appeal to the Hjan.

"Are you ready to return south?" she asked.

Guya frowned. They had avoided discussing it before now, but after she'd forced him to fight, it seemed appropriate that she *did* speak of it with him.

"I know enough to fear the Hjan."

It wasn't an answer, which meant he hadn't decided. "We haven't seen any sign of the Hjan since leaving Wesjan and having the accords signed."

"No sign of them doesn't mean that they have gone quietly." Guya squeezed the wheel with more intensity than was necessary, but Carth could not blame him given all that they had been through and seen today.

He had come away from the fights with injuries to his leg and his arm, which she had bandaged and covered with a mixture of herbs her mother had once taught her. It would staunch the bleeding and might prevent them from getting infected, but would likely do nothing more than that. It would certainly not speed up the recovery.

For his sake, she wished there were some way to help him recover quickly, the same way she had with her magic.

"No. That's my fear as well."

"Once we reach Lonsyn, what do you intend to do?" he asked.

"I had thought to continue sailing, searching for answers. I'm afraid there are more questions now."

As he stared out at the sea, his face took on a haunted expression. "One of the things I've learned sailing is that there are always more questions. Each land has different stories, rumors of sorts, and each land seems to have its own sort of power. In the north, you have the power of the shadows and of the flame. In the south, there is a different sort of power. There is a city where the men all have green eyes and all have abilities unlike any other. To the west, you have those who can mix herbs and medicines in ways that draw power. Who is to say what can happen when you look to the east or further to the south?"

Carth watched him, expecting a joke or some other comment, but he made none. His words were edged with almost a hint of anger, though Carth suspected she misinterpreted it. She had seen a green-eyed man one time, but he had come with the Hjan.

"I haven't told you much about my parents," Carth said.

"Only that your father was Reshian."

She grunted. "Reshian. Would that it were so simple." Silence settled between them for a moment before she dared breaking it. "They were of Ih-lash, a land that is no more."

"You've told me that. I haven't been that far to the north in years. Even then, there were rumors they were fading."

"They didn't fade. They were destroyed. They probably couldn't do anything against the Hjan."

"The shadows are powerful."

"You haven't seen the Hjan fight. You haven't seen how quickly they can kill, as if you were nothing more than an insect to them." She noted that Guya tensed but said nothing. Was it possible he knew more about the Hjan than she had realized? "My father possesses the power of the shadows, likely shadow born like myself. My mother must have the power of the A'ras flame. She must be descended from Lashasn, though she never spoke of it. They both left."

"You said they wanted you to train with the A'ras."

"I don't know why they brought me to Nyaesh. Before coming there, I knew nothing of powers and magic, only that some had power and others did not." She leaned on the railing, letting the sensation of the shadows around her fill her with power. "Do you know that I feared the A'ras when we first came to Nyaesh?"

Guya grunted and laughed. "Many fear them. And for good reason."

Carth thought about what she had seen when she was a child, the fear she'd felt when she'd first encountered the A'ras. That fear had been nothing compared to the fear she'd felt when seeing the man smearing the blood of his victims across his chest and somehow gaining powers that should not be.

How much blood must they have spilled?

The sails were stained with red, and their clothing was stained with red.

Dozens would have died. Dozens of dozens.

A village.

"You think of them again," Guya said.

She could only nod. "They were able to ignore the connection to the shadows."

"Aye."

"But not to the flame."

"I fear that will make them even more dangerous," Guya noted.

It wasn't the danger that she feared. If there was a way to stop them, Carth could do it. The challenge was that there were others who sought power, and if they could get ahold of power like that, what else might they do? How might they use that against the Reshian or others? What responsibility did she have to stop them?

"I need to find them," she said softly.

"Find them and do what? What would you do that would stop this kind of magic alone?"

"If we don't—"

Guya placed his hand on her shoulder. Callused fingers gripped her shoulder and he squeezed. "There will always be another power, and then another. How many do you think you can stop?"

"I—"

"You forged peace between the A'ras and the Reshian. I come from the south, and even I know how important that was... and how difficult. But there will be another. And another. Each time, you run the risk of others with power."

Guya was right, but why was it that it still troubled her that there was power like that out there? What was it particularly that bothered her? Was it the actual blood magic? That had been bad enough, but she didn't think that was what it was.

If she was forced to put an answer to it, she knew that it was because of the Hjan.

What had Invar said about them?

They were collectors of power.

This kind of power, that which would use the blood of others to fuel the magic, was just the kind of thing the Hjan would want. That was the reason she *had* to ensure they didn't acquire it.

But how?

It was only her, Dara, and Guya. They were not enough to stop the Hjan.

"It's more than the Hjan," she said to herself.

Guya nodded, his face solemn. "Aye. It is."

If she didn't do something, there were other villages like the one they had seen, and there were others like Dara who would suffer, all in the pursuit of power.

Was there anything that *she* could do?

She didn't want power, but she had it.

Didn't that place a certain responsibility upon her shoulders?

With a sigh, she stared out over the water, trying to come to a decision. For her to be able to do more, she would need more help. It would have to be about more than only Carth, more than stopping the Hjan. That had been important, but there was more she could do.

First, she had to understand her abilities.

That meant the Reshian.

No… if she were honest with herself, that meant both the Reshian *and* the A'ras.

Which meant they had other stops to make.

She nodded, mostly to herself.

"What have you decided?" Guya asked.

"First we stop in Lonsyn, then… then it's time I return to my past."

He frowned. "Why your past?"

"Because I need to understand what I can do—what I can *really* do—if I'm to be able to do anything to stop these kinds of attacks."

Guya nodded. "It's about time. I will go with you, Carthenne Rel. For this, I will go with you."

CHAPTER 7

THE CITY OF LONSYN WAS LIKE MANY OF THE PORT CITIES they'd visited since leaving Wesjan. There was the noise of dockworkers, all calling to each other, many trying to outdo the next, trying either to get the best price on fish or to pull men toward taverns. Other noise came from the city itself, this a mixture of sounds all congealed together, making it so that she couldn't differentiate one from another. The smells were the same, the air filled with the stink of fish and grain, but there were other scents here too, many she couldn't place.

As much like other ports as it was, there was something different about it as well. From Guya, Carth knew it was a busy port, and one that smugglers favored. That made it dangerous in ways the others had not been.

Long fingers of wooden docks stretched into the harbor, allowing Guya to sail much closer to shore than he would otherwise have been able to do. His eyes scanned the crowds with the same nervous suspicion he displayed at every port.

The *Goth Spald* cruised toward the docks and anchored in the harbor. Without more of a crew, they weren't able to row closer to shore and had to take the dinghy the rest of the way.

"Is it safe to leave her out here alone?" Carth asked. "I could stay…"

Guya looked up at the ship with a nervous glance. "It should be. Lonsyn is a trading port, but there are enough disreputable types here that could come after an empty ship."

"I could hide it in the shadows."

"You'd do that?"

Carth shrugged. "I would try. I can't say whether it would work all that well, or whether I could hold on to it."

Guya shook his head. "Then don't bother trying. You might need your strength here, especially if we intend to find answers."

"Where would you have us go?" Dara asked.

"There are a few different taverns we could try," Guya suggested. "If our intent is to find answers, then we'd want to start along the docks."

"Do you think we'll find anything in the taverns?" Dara asked.

Carth actually smiled. She hadn't spent much time in taverns since she was younger, but she had a certain fondness for them. There was the gaming, and the laughter, and the noise, all of which belonged in the taverns. Add to that the mix of foods and other things you would find there… she could almost taste Vera's cooking.

"We'll find something there," she said.

Dara shrugged. "If you say so."

They motioned for Guya to lead and he started down the street and along the docks. He moved quickly and seemed to have a tavern in mind. When they stopped at it, the tavern was practically empty, only a few people inside. He backed out and shook his head. "Not this one, then."

They tried a few other places, but each place was much like the first, all mostly empty other than a few serving girls and a barkeep. They weren't the kind of places you'd get answers. They would be more likely to stand out, which none of them wanted.

By the time they reached the Grand Hack, Carth had begun to suspect they wouldn't find anything at all.

As they opened the door, something left her skin tingling, the hairs on her arms standing on end. There was something off here.

Carth studied the interior of the tavern. One hand gripped the hilt of her sword, though she didn't expect to need it, not here and not with the others she had with her. Shadows licked along the sides of the tavern, probably too faint for others to see, but Carth felt them as much as she saw them.

"What is it, Carth?" Dara asked.

Carth tipped her head to the side, focusing on the irritant she felt, something that crawled along the surface of her skin. She wasn't able to explain what it was she felt, only that something was wrong. "There was power here. Enough that I can detect."

"You can detect both Reshian and A'ras. Which is it?"

Dara asked. In the days since the attack, Dara had been reserved and hadn't said much.

"I don't know. Neither, as far as I can tell."

She stepped into the tavern and realized not only had power been here, but something else had. Carth embraced the shadows and—thinking about the blood magic—added the power of the flame as well.

A body lay in front of her. There were others around here as well, all lying unmoving. How many had died here? Who had killed them?

She paused in front of the first. He was a stocky man with a bald head and a long brown robe that likely signified some sort of religious person. In the islands, it was difficult to know.

She sniffed the air, not expecting to find anything.

"Was this the Hjan?" Dara asked.

"I can't tell," Carth said. It didn't feel right. This wasn't how the Hjan operated, or how they attacked. "The accords would protect this place."

"The accords are only with the Hjan," Dara said.

"And the Reshian and A'ras," Carth said, leaning over the next body she'd come to. This was an older woman whose throat had been cut, leaving her to bleed out onto the ground. It was fresh—or relatively so—as the blood hadn't completely congealed. "But this wasn't the Hjan."

"How can you be sure?" Dara asked, turning her irritation from Guya onto Carth.

"Were it the Hjan, I would have detected them."

Dara sniffed and slammed her knife back into her sheath. "You claim you would have detected them, but you didn't know what was on those ships."

"No," Carth said, looking up at her. "I didn't. But I've seen no sign that the Hjan have violated the accords."

Without a violation, Carth wouldn't do anything to disrupt the peace, especially since they had fought so hard to gain it in the first place. In this, she agreed with Dara: the Hjan likely planned something more than they knew, which was the very reason Carth worried about the blood magic.

Guya stopped next to her, crouching low as she studied the dead woman. "This was not the Hjan. You think it's—"

Carth shook her head. "I don't know. It's different than the ship, but it might be the same."

"Can you tell if there's anything else here?"

"Such as other powers?"

Guya nodded. "You've said you can pick up on the Hjan. If it's not them, are there others you *can* detect?"

"Some, but I don't detect anything else."

"Why do I get the sense that bothers you?"

"Because it does. That blood magic… I wouldn't be able to detect it."

Carth stood and surveyed the rest of the tavern. There were at least a dozen other bodies, each lying in various positions, and all with their throats slit, making it appear as if it had been a non-magical attack. That didn't change the softly burning sense she had across her skin, and the sense of unease that crawled within her that this wasn't quite right.

"How many different powers can you detect?"

"Reshian. A'ras. Hjan. I don't know about any others." Now that she knew about the blood magic, could she detect it? If she could, would she be able to anticipate it, and maybe defend against it?

She moved to the next body. There was nothing particularly interesting about this one either, other than the fact that this was a younger man, probably barely older than a boy, and his neck now had a gaping wound where his life had leaked out.

"We don't know what's taking place here."

"We don't, but that's what I need to discover."

She'd gone from having her parents teaching and protecting her, to Vera and Hal, to the A'ras, and then to Jhon. After escaping Ras, she had discovered she didn't need someone else watching her, and didn't need for someone to guide her. She was able to make her own decisions.

After stopping the Hjan threat, it was clear to her what she needed to do, if not *how*.

"You think this a magical attack?" Dara asked, touching the back of her neck. She made a point of not looking at the bodies.

"I do. When I use my different abilities, I can feel something. With the A'ras magic, it's an irritant. With the shadows, it's something off, as if the shadows are distorted. With this… I can't put my finger on it, but there's something not quite right," she said.

She stopped at the counter running along one side of the tavern. The layout here reminded her in some ways of the Wounded Lyre, the tavern where she had spent the better part of a year after her parents had died—her mother, at least. Her father lived, something that troubled her still.

A film coated the counter, and she ran her hand along it, finding it sticky. Was it only dried ale and spilled food, or was there something else here?

Why kill all these people? *Had* it been the same kind of attack they'd encountered on the sea?

"*Is* it them?" Dara asked. "The blood priests?"

"Priests?"

Dara shrugged. "You described them as using the blood in something like a ceremony. That's the only term that seems to fit."

Strangely, it did for Carth as well. "I don't know."

She made her way around the inside of the tavern. She stopped at each of the bodies, looking at them, but she detected nothing else. Each person had been killed in the same way.

That troubled her.

"Why would all of their throats be slit?" she asked, looking to Guya for answers she doubted he had. "They didn't kill the women this way."

"Not all of these are women," Guya said.

Not all women, so the attack *wasn't* like what they'd come across on the *Tempar*.

But there was something else that troubled her. There was blood, but not so much as she would have expected. The tavern itself didn't appear as if it had been attacked, so there didn't seem to have been much of a struggle. No chairs were tipped over, and tables still had trays laden with food on them. Whatever had happened here had been deliberate, and it had been done almost casually, not with the kind of violence these deaths should require.

Had they already been dead?

That would explain why there didn't seem to have been a struggle, and it might explain why there didn't seem to be nearly as much blood as she would expect.

And nothing answered the question of whether there had been a power used here. That was the question she needed answered most of all.

"What are you thinking?" Dara asked.

"They were already dead," Carth said, standing and taking a deep breath, peering around the tavern. What had she missed? What more would she be able to find?

"How do you know?"

"I don't know, but it is the answer that makes the most sense."

Carth finished her circuit of the inside of the tavern. There wasn't anything more to it other than this single room and a kitchen in the back. In Nyaesh, many of the taverns also possessed an inn, but this one didn't.

She stepped back out into the sunlight. There was a time when having nothing but the bright sun overhead would have posed a problem, but that had been when her primary strength had come in the form of the shadow magic. Now that she wore her mother's ring, she was better able to connect to the A'ras flame and no longer struggled to reach even that level of power. The sunlight didn't necessarily help, but it didn't restrict her either.

Dara followed her out of the tavern. They stood on the edge of the city, and the docks stretched away from the shore, long teeth reaching into the deepwater bay. There weren't many like it that could accommodate ships like the *Goth Spald*, but this city could.

In either direction down the street, other buildings

rose. Many were two or three stories tall, something she had grown accustomed to seeing on these islands, especially as they often had such little usable land. The city attempted to make full use of what they had available.

"What is it?" Dara asked. The anger in her voice remained. How long would that be there?

"This tavern is like this, but no one else seemed to know."

"If they didn't go in…"

"Why wouldn't they have gone in?" Carth asked. "Look at the street. It's not as if it isn't busy."

There were hundreds of people moving along the street. Most were dressed in the same thick wool, though some had robes like the man she'd seen in the tavern. As she watched the street, she noted people moving into some of the storefront buildings and others back out. Even the stores on either side of the tavern had people entering and leaving, but not the tavern.

Could it only be their presence?

She grabbed Dara and pulled her across the street. They stopped in a shadowed section between two buildings and Carth pulled on the shadows, concealing them. As she did, she watched, waiting to see what else might come out.

Guya emerged, and she released the shadows enough for him to see them before engulfing him in shadows as well. He'd had enough time with her to recognize what she did, and didn't question it until he'd crossed the street and reached them.

"Why are you concealing us?" he asked.

"There's something here—"

Nausea hit her and she stopped talking.

It was a quick flickering sense, one that nearly bent her over with nausea. It had been nearly a year since she'd detected something similar, but she knew immediately what it was.

"They're here."

"Who?" Guya asked.

Dara watched her, a worried look on her face. Carth had explained what it meant when she detected the nausea, and she seemed to understand without her telling them. But Guya needed answers.

"The Hjan," Carth said. "They're here."

CHAPTER 8

Carth pulled on the shadows as she crossed the street, gliding with them. There had been a time when she hadn't known how to move and hold the shadows at the same time, but she'd discovered that she could do so by flowing with them. This allowed her the ability to slide with them and even on a bright day, she could use the shadows as she crossed the street, pulling something that appeared more like smoke or fog as she did.

She reached the door of the tavern, her sword unsheathed, and kicked open the door.

On the other side, three Hjan stood.

They all turned to her as she entered, two with the same strange scar running down the side of her face as she'd seen with the others, and focused on her. The third had no scar, and focused on her with eyes that were the deepest green she'd ever seen.

"You would violate the accords?" she asked.

The unscarred man waved a hand and the other two

disappeared with a flicker. Carth noted they took two of the bodies with them.

She frowned. What was this about?

Her Tsatsun training kicked in. The Hjan would have an agenda, and if she could figure it out, she would know what their endgame might be. The trouble was, she didn't know what they wanted this time. Before, it had been about obtaining the power of the Reshian or the A'ras, but these lands didn't know either of those powers. Whatever the reason they were here, it would be about power—Carth was sure of that—but what power existed here?

Could it be about the blood magic? Had the Hjan learned of it already?

"There is no violation unless you attack, Carthenne of Ih-lash," he said.

She hesitated. The Hjan knew her name. She'd expected that they would learn, hadn't really expected to keep that secret from them, but that they knew it placed her in a more dangerous position. She knew nothing about this man, other than that he was one of the Hjan.

"Were you responsible for this?"

The Hjan grunted, somehow making it sound like a laugh. "Responsible for this? You have seen how the Hjan work, Carthenne of Ih-lash."

"That was no answer."

"This was not us."

"Then why are you here?"

The Hjan shrugged and then flickered, appearing again near the back of the tavern. As she watched, he flickered from place to place around the tavern before finally settling on one of the dead. It was an older man, and not one she'd spent much time studying.

"I would ask the same of you," he said.

"I'm here to ensure you don't violate the accords."

The green-eyed man smiled. "The accords have been signed by all parties. Why would we violate them? Besides, unless you claim membership with the Reshian or A'ras, I think you are outside of the accords, are you not?"

He knew.

That had been part of the reason she'd remained free from the Reshian and from the A'ras. If she joined either, she wouldn't be able to act were the Hjan to attack again, and she *wanted* to be able to attack them. She'd seen the way her combination of magic, both the shadows and the flame, allowed her to stop the Hjan. There were few others with that ability.

"I have not attacked you. Do not entice me to do so," the Hjan said.

"If I were going to attack you, I would have done so by now."

The green-eyed man smiled at her. "So confident. I must admit you have proven an intriguing challenge. It is too bad you've neglected the *other* parties in the accords."

"What other parties?"

"You have forgotten them already? And here I heard you were half of each."

"The Reshian and the A'ras maintain the peace."

"Do they?" he asked with a smile.

Carth felt her heart speeding up. She'd remained

outside of the accords, but what would happen if the Hjan forced either of the other parties to violate them?

"What happens if I drive my sword through your stomach?"

His smile widened. "You would risk the peace you so graciously established?"

"I would risk nothing."

"No? The Hjan would claim Reshian attacked. Or A'ras. Perhaps we could even place the blame on the C'than, though I do not believe you have accepted their offer. I imagine the Trivant are most displeased with that decision."

Carth forced herself to maintain a neutral expression. How did this man know so much about her? And what were the C'than and the Trivant?

More she didn't understand.

But if he knew what he claimed, he would be able to use it not only against her, but against those she would see remain safe. The accords had settled the Reshian and the A'ras, stopping a silent war that had been waged far longer than she once would ever have believed.

Carth had seen this man before, she was sure of it, and now that he had come here openly… or had he?

She had surprised him by coming here, and he had the other Hjan removing bodies. There had to be some reason behind it.

"How much do you know about blood magic?" Carth asked.

The green-eyed man offered a hint of a smile. "I know more than you can imagine, Carthenne of Ih-lash."

She lunged at him, slicing with her sword, not

intending to hit him, but wanting to distract more than anything. With the attack, she pulled on the shadows, drawing them with her, wrapping herself in them for strength.

The green-eyed man flickered.

When he reappeared, he held a slender blade. "You would risk the accords for revenge?"

"Is that what you think?" Carth attacked again, this time nearly catching him. When he flickered, the nausea was stronger.

He appeared in the same place he had been before. "It's a dangerous game you're playing, Carthenne of Ih-lash."

"What makes you think this is a game?"

"Is not everything a game?"

He watched her expression, and Carth didn't think she managed to keep it nearly as neutral as she wanted.

How much did he know about her?

Did he know that her father had played games with her? Did he know about her collecting scraps while living along the docks with Vera and Hal, the way they had made a game of it for her? Did he know that she had learned Tsatsun from Ras?

He seemed to understand her struggle, and smiled again.

Carth lunged, pulling on both the shadows and the S'al.

Now that she wore her mother's ring, she could use that power in ways she could not before. It was as if the ring itself connected her to the magic more deeply, allowing her to reach for the flame without the same anger and passion that she'd needed before.

She pressed out with her power, pushing away from her in an attack, no longer using her sword.

The green-eyed man waved his hand, and the power seemed to dissolve around him.

In some ways, the control of power he possessed reminded her of Ras, but what this man did was different from what Ras did. He used no obvious magic, none that she could see. He'd simply stopped her.

Stranger still, she'd felt nothing when he had. Not as she had when she had fought the Hjan before.

Wasn't this man one of the Hjan?

"Who are you?" she asked.

The green-eyed man grinned. "I thought you knew."

She had thought she knew, just as she had thought that she could defeat him, but with the power he possessed, she wouldn't be able to overwhelm him with her abilities. In that way, it reminded her of how Ras had defeated her, the way he had managed to simply wave off her attack, and worse, block her from even reaching her magic.

"You're with the Hjan."

"The Hjan are a tool, Carthenne of Ih-lash. Much like you are used as a tool."

"I'm not used by anyone."

"No? Then why are you here?"

Carth didn't have to answer, and didn't know why she did. She hoped that keeping him talking would get him to reveal more about himself, and she needed to understand his abilities, needed to know *who* he was. "Partly prevent the Hjan from disrupting the accords. That is all you want."

"Is that what you think, Carthenne of Ih-lash? Is that what they have taught you?"

"Tell me what it might be, then."

Wrapped in the shadows, she slid toward him, attacking again.

The green-eyed man flickered almost lazily away from her, a wide smile on his face.

When he reappeared, he watched her. "Have you asked them how we are so different?"

"Asked who?"

The green-eyed man flickered again as she lunged toward him. She no longer thought she could stop him, and if he truly attacked her, she wondered if she would be able to defeat him. The only hope she had was that he seemed interested in remaining away from her sword, and his gaze occasionally drifted to her knife.

Switching weapons, she held the knife out in front of her, slipping her sword back into the sheath. If he feared the knife more than the sword, she would use that instead.

And why wouldn't he? When she'd faced the Hjan in Wesjan, she'd used the knife and forced shadows through it, using the power of the shadows and of the flame to stop the Hjan. She wondered if she might be able to do something similar to him. With the way he made a point of staying away from her knife, she suspected he did as well.

"You have much to learn before you can play the real game."

"What game is that?"

"The only one that matters," he said, flickering again.

Carth noted that he appeared near the same body he had before. She glanced down at the man, trying to understand why he would continue to return to this body, but didn't see anything that would help her.

"What game?" she asked. She lunged, knife extended, shadows flowing through her.

He grabbed the arm of the dead man. "Power." Then he flickered, disappearing.

Nausea rolled through her again, slowly settling back to nothingness.

The door to the tavern opened again, and Dara entered with her knife unsheathed, Guya following. There was hesitancy to their faces, but they had come. That pleased her more than it should. "What was it? Why did you hurry back?"

"They were here," she answered.

"They violated the accords for this?" Dara said.

"There was no battle."

"And therefore no violation," Guya said.

Carth flushed, wondering if the Hjan would use her attack to signal a violation of the accords. She had been the one responsible for implementing them. If they failed *because* of her, what would be the point of all that she had done?

"That doesn't change the fact that they came here at the same time as these attacks took place," Dara said.

Carth stared at the ground. Holding on to the shadows and the flame as she did, she thought to detect whether there was anything here that would explain the Hjan's interest in certain of the bodies.

"Carth?" Dara asked.

"They wanted something. I don't know what it was. And he implied the Reshian and the A'ras might violate the accords."

"The Hjan weren't attacking?" Guya asked.

"This wasn't them," Carth said. She still didn't know who might have done this, but it wasn't the Hjan. And if it wasn't them, then she needed to understand.

"If not them, then we don't need to get involved," Guya said.

Dara said something more, but Carth ignored it. They were after something, and she didn't know what it was, but she needed to. With the Hjan, the fact that they were here at all was reason enough for her to worry.

She focused on the bodies the Hjan had ignored. When she'd arrived, he'd been near the man dressed in the robes, and then he had flickered around the room, stopping at several others. Was there anything about those others she could discover? If she could, would she be able to find out what the Hjan wanted from them?

Carth made her way from body to body again, but there wasn't anything different about them.

They would be about power. That much wouldn't change, she didn't think.

Her mind started working through the different possibilities, piecing together how the Hjan would play it out, but she couldn't come up with anything. She didn't know enough. The only answer was to find more information.

With the Hjan, that placed her in a difficult situation, especially if she was always a step or two behind. To play Tsatsun, and to win, she needed to know as much about the game board as she could. With the Hjan, it was as if they intended to obscure part of the playing surface from her.

"What do we do?" Dara asked.

"We need to find more information."

"About the Hjan?" Dara asked.

"The Hjan. This attack. Those on the ships. Everything."

The place to start was where she had planned to go anyway—the place where everything had changed for her. To find a way to understand Ih-lash and the Reshian, she needed to go to Odian and Ras. Only then did she think she could move forward.

CHAPTER 9

Carth hadn't returned to Odian since she'd been imprisoned here. The ship was the same, and traveling on the *Spald* with Guya left her with memories of her escape from Nyaesh, back when she'd feared what the Hjan intended, and back when she'd believed her abilities with shadow and flame would protect her. Ras had proven how little she actually knew.

They arrived in the city in the daylight. Even then, the sky was thick with clouds that blocked the sunlight, creating a gloomy appearance. Thunder rumbled distantly, a vague sort of sound that gave only an indistinct sense of a coming storm.

Dara and Guya waited on the ship for her. Both could come into Odian, but neither had the desire. That surprised Carth. She would have expected Dara to be interested in meeting Ras, but she was not. At least, not yet.

Carth surveyed the street, noting a dozen or so people

who made their way along the street, many traveling to the docks and to other ships moored in the deepwater harbor. She paused at a tavern, thinking back to when she'd spied Guya the first time, before continuing onward. Ras would not be found in the city.

There was a part of her that wondered whether she could find him at all. The man was secretive and had somehow managed to hide his home from her within moments of her leaving it. She might have developed greater skill with the shadows and with the A'ras magic, but she still felt like the younger version of herself, who had been so easily overpowered. The only difference was the knowledge she'd gained working with Ras.

Outside the city, she followed a path along the rocks before cutting inland. Carth pulled on the shadows as she went, the overcast day making this easier, and the shadows likely necessary in order for her to find him. He would likely detect her use of the shadows, and would come find her. If he was willing.

She approached a flat section of land. This should be where she'd find Ras, if he remained near Odian. Carth didn't know if he would after what had happened with the Hjan.

A soft presence pulsed near her, and she spun.

She didn't expect an attack here, and now that she knew more about Ras, she didn't fear that he would try to harm her, but she also didn't think she'd be able to easily defeat him if he did. In many ways, he was more capable than her, and he certainly had a greater control of his ability than she did. They shared the power of the S'al, but only Ras really knew how to use it. With it, he had managed to counter her connection to the shadows as well as to the A'ras magic.

Ras stood opposite her, arms crossed over his chest. He was a thin man with silver hair and a long face, but it wasn't his physical size that had brought her back. It was his mind. "Carth of Ih-lash," Ras said.

"Ras Ahtharn."

"Why have you brought violence to my shores?"

She held her hand toward him, open-palmed. "No violence. Only me, Ras. I came alone."

"Why?"

"For knowledge and understanding."

He snorted. "You have proven you can outplay me, Carth of Ih-lash. There is nothing more I can teach of Tsatsun."

She hadn't really thought that would be what he could teach, and that wasn't what she needed from him. What she needed was to understand how to play when she couldn't see the game. She needed to understand why the Hjan would have gone to Lonsyn and what they might use the blood priests for when she couldn't determine it from their moves.

"The Hjan remain active," she said.

"The accords will only restrain them for so long. It was an interesting move, but one that will ultimately fail."

"Why?"

"Because of what the Hjan seek. They search for power, and they would take it from those who possess it. What you have done is restrain them from reaching those who have confounded them to this point. How long do you think you'll be able to do that?"

Carth met his steely gaze. "As long as I must. If there is no one else willing to block the Hjan from reaching us, and from attacking, then it has to be me."

Ras turned away from her and stared into the distance. Did he search for his home? There was no evidence of it here, and with whatever he had used to obscure it, she didn't detect it with the shadows or with the A'ras magic.

"Why did you come back, Carth of Ih-lash?"

"I need to know how to play when you can't see the game."

"You would still believe this is all a game that can be won?"

"I think the Hjan want power and to destroy those with it. You taught me that Tsatsun allows an understanding of strategy, but I've only played when I knew the game and the pieces. I need to find a way to play when those are hidden from me."

"The Hjan do not play the same game as you."

"Then help me understand the game they *do* play."

Ras started forward and waved his hand. Carth followed, cresting a small rise to find Ras's home on the other side.

"Come inside, and we'll see what I can still teach you."

Ras sat across from her, the game board between them. His brow was knitted in concentration as they played a traditional game of Tsatsun. Carth had maneuvered him into a place without options, and it was only a matter of time before the game would be over. When it was, it would be the second time she'd beaten him.

It had been a while since she'd played a difficult game, but in the time since she'd last faced Ras, her skill had improved. So had his, but it wasn't the same.

She watched the way he continued playing, persisting in spite of the fact that she had a counter to every move he had remaining. He slid his Huntress forward, and she claimed it. The next was one of the remaining Dalyns. She claimed that as well. He had only a Wolfian left, and she surrounded it.

Finally, Ras sat back. "It has been many years since I have been so soundly defeated. How long ago was it that you knew it was over?"

"It doesn't matter."

Ras took a deep breath and began replacing the pieces on the board, this time setting up only one side. "It *does* matter. How long ago were you aware of my technique?"

Carth debated: should she tell the truth, or should she avoid hurting his feelings with it?

"Nearly twenty moves ago," she admitted.

Ras shook his head. "Not simply defeated. If you were anticipating this twenty moves prior, there would be no way I could have countered."

"You taught me well."

"I didn't teach you this. What you exhibit is nothing like I can teach."

She didn't want to argue, but this was exactly what he'd taught her. By holding her in prison, he had forced her to come up with a strategy in which she would play as if she were every other person she knew. Eventually, that became a melding of styles, and now... now it was the only way she could play.

"Are you saying you can't help me learn how to stop the Hjan?"

Ras motioned to the board. "What do you see?"

"You've only placed half of the pieces."

"Correct. That is why you're here, isn't it? You want to know how you can win when you can't see the moves the other person is making?" She nodded. "Imagine what you would do if you couldn't see what I would do. How did you anticipate twenty moves ahead to defeat me?"

"I saw the way you arranged the pieces, and I calculated the possible moves you might make."

"With Tsatsun, that would have been... hundreds— perhaps thousands—at that point."

Carth nodded.

Ras leaned forward. "Good. For you to do what you would like with the Hjan, you will have to do the same, but you will have to plan dozens of moves in advance. Possibly more. That will leave you with thousands upon thousands of possibilities."

Carth thought about the problem. Sitting with Ras made it easier for her to talk it through, but she still didn't see the solution. "Adding what I learn will allow me to adjust."

He nodded. "With the Hjan, you might collect only fragments, nothing more than scraps of information."

She smiled at his use of the word. "I can collect scraps if that's what it will take."

"You will have to, or you won't know where they really move."

The idea of collecting information the same way she had once collected scraps appealed to her, as did the need to piece together what she had learned so she could discover the next move the Hjan might make. She knew what they'd done in the past, and how they had attacked the northern continent, and she had seen their interest in those dead in Lonsyn, but what she didn't have was other pieces of information.

"What do you fear they will do?" Ras asked.

"That's just it. I don't know what they might do. They've attacked in the north, and they attempted to coordinate another attack, pitting the remnants of Ih and those of Lashasn against each other. What if they do something similar?" The offhanded comment about the other parties to the accords violating them troubled her. Was that how they were using the blood priests?

"Reshian and the A'ras now watch the north. Do you fear you wouldn't hear from them if there were something more?"

Carth suspected that she would hear if the Hjan returned. Maybe not directly, but the C'than had enough people situated throughout the north that there shouldn't be an issue with discovering another attack, and then sending word.

What she needed was more information about the Hjan. What she needed was to head south.

"I see you have decided," Ras said.

"Is that what you've wanted from me from the beginning?"

Ras shook his head. "It's not about what I want."

"Then what?" When he didn't answer, she pressed. "What are the C'than?"

"Where did you hear that term?"

"From the Hjan."

Ras closed his eyes and took a slow breath. "You draw dangerous enemies, Carthenne Rel. Or perhaps dangerous allies."

"What are they?"

"They are powerful, and they might be the only power able to hold the Hjan accountable."

"Assassins?"

Ras shrugged. "Some. Not all."

"Then what?"

"They are seekers of knowledge. Much like you, I presume, though they do so with intent whereas you have seemed to do so accidentally. They are skilled in ways that I can't even see."

Skilled. That worried her. Was that another type of magic, much like what Guya suggested? "Would they try to use me?"

"Perhaps. Or would they simply choose you?"

Carth sighed. She thought they would share with her, but she didn't really know if they would. "Do you serve them?"

Ras studied his Tsatsun board and shook his head.

"Why not? With your talent, wouldn't they want to use you as well?"

"The C'than never wanted me. They wanted the idea of me, Carth of Ih-lash."

"Do you think they want the same from me?"

"I believe they have another use for you."

"What sort of use?"

Ras turned his attention to the board. "There are times when you know nothing, when you feel as if you're stuck in the shadows."

"I work in the shadows, Ras."

"Not like this. With these shadows, you may have an idea of light, a hint of movement, but you remain uncertain. That is the C'than. They—much like the Hjan—prefer to operate in the darkness."

"If I learn to play one-sided for the Hjan, I'll learn what I need for the C'than as well?"

"I don't know. They have different motives."

"What kind of motives?"

"The kind where they want to use me. Perhaps they want to use you as well. You would do well to understand what they want of you, Carth of Ih-lash, before you become Carthenne of the C'than."

She sighed, moving a piece and beginning to play a game where she moved against an invisible foe. The game was less interesting, but more difficult. If the opponent could attack from anywhere and nowhere, how did she know if the game even continued?

Ras disappeared for a while before returning with a pitcher of tea, which he set between them. "Rest, Carth of Ih-lash. Share a mug of tea with me as we play another game of Tsatsun. Then you will depart."

CHAPTER 10

After she beat Ras a third time, they sat quietly in Ras's game room. There had been a sense of resignation from him about midway through the game, shortly after the time when she had seen all the possibilities for him to win, and knew the counter.

They shared a cup of tea—something she hadn't done when she'd been with him the last time—and sat quietly, the silence giving Carth a chance to reflect on the game, and the strategy she'd used.

Somehow, she would have to find scraps of information so she could anticipate what the Hjan might do next, only she wasn't entirely certain where to begin, or how.

She could use the C'than, but she hadn't decided what her role with them would be. First, she wanted to be better prepared. Jhon might observe her, but she had spent the same amount of time observing him.

Perhaps she had already begun playing a different kind

of game without realizing it. Maybe that was what Ras wanted her to see.

"You haven't told me why you never worked with the C'than."

Ras set his tea down. "You know the Wanderer, but how many others within the C'than have you met?"

"The Wanderer?"

"The man you call Jhon. The Wanderer. He serves the C'than."

That made a certain sort of sense. Had he been playing her when he had come to Nyaesh?

"It seems he wasn't exactly forthcoming with who he served."

He smiled. "There is an advantage to playing your pieces close as they do. Others cannot read you easily, and you are better able to surprise with your next move."

"You don't trust them."

"What is trust, Carth of Ih-lash? I see them as a lesser evil than the Hjan. They would still choose to manipulate me, if they were able. Had you not intervened with the Hjan, I think they might have succeeded."

She had a hard time believing that anyone would be able to manipulate him. "Do any of the Trivant play Tsatsun?" She gambled on the term, but had heard it from the Hjan and suspected it mattered.

"You listen, don't you, Carthenne Rel?"

"I observe."

"More than any I have ever taught." He took up his tea and sipped. "I often wonder if we aren't playing a game the Trivant have established."

Wouldn't Jhon have said something to her? Probably

not. He wanted her to join him and work with the C'than, claiming there would be more to her training that she could accomplish by working with them, and until she did, she doubted he would be forthcoming about the intentions of the C'than.

"Would you join them?" Ras asked her.

"I know nothing about them."

"If you learned, would you?"

"You said they were powerful."

"Very."

"That means they observed the Hjan when they could have done something."

"What would you have had them do?"

Carth turned so she could see him clearly. "The Hjan killed many people because they worked to position others. They hurt countless others."

"You mean they hurt you."

Carth swallowed before nodding slowly.

"Did you not tell me your father still lives?"

"He lives. And leads the Reshian."

She hadn't discovered whether he was shadow born like her or only shadow blessed. For him to lead the Reshian made it likely he was shadow born. If that was the case, why hadn't he stayed and taught her? Why had he abandoned her to Nyaesh, trusting that she would manage on her own?

As much as anything, those were questions she wanted answered, but they were questions she wasn't sure she would find the answers to.

"You could return to him and ask the questions that plague you."

"I cannot."

"You fear the Reshian?"

Carth shook her head. "I don't fear the Reshian, much as I don't fear the A'ras. I don't belong to either."

"You belong to both, Carth of Ih-lash. You are born of both, perhaps more than any other."

"Which is why I can't return."

"You talk in circles," Ras said.

"The Hjan seek power. That won't change. The accords hold them for now, but they are between the A'ras, the Reshian, and the Hjan. Not with me."

"As you intentionally established."

She smiled. Ras had seen it as well as the green-eyed man. What sort of Tsatsun player would he have been?

"You would destroy them?"

"I would keep the Hjan from harming others. I will destroy them if necessary."

Ras nodded slowly. "Do you really think you can do this yourself?"

"I don't know."

Ras sat back. "Let me tell you what I know about them, add to your scraps of information." He offered a hint of a smile as he said it. *Did* he know that was what Vera had called it? "The Hjan are an arm of another group. They call themselves scholars, and possess a tower of learning in the far south. They use power, collect it much like a child might collect seashells."

"I've seen that."

He shook his head. "You've seen the Hjan. They are the… assassin, I suppose you would call it, arm of these scholars. They are the ones sent to find those with power, and discover ways to subdue it. The others will collect it. Hold it. Study it."

"The Hjan didn't seem interested in collecting power when they were in Nyaesh."

Ras's eyes clouded. "No. There was something different afoot there, though I wasn't able to determine what it was."

"Who is the green-eyed man?" He knew about her, and she needed to learn what she could about him. From what she'd seen, he appeared to lead the Hjan, but had no scar, nothing like the others of the Hjan possessed, the marker of what she suspected gave them their power.

"Green-eyed? There are many of the Hjan who have green eyes."

"There's one," she said. "He was there during the attack near Wesjan. He was in Lonsyn when we found the bodies. I think he leads the Hjan."

Ras clasped his hands together on his lap. "I haven't found any who lead the Hjan, Carthenne of Ih-lash. If you have discovered this man, then you are one step ahead of me."

"You've faced them longer than I have. When did you first encounter them?"

Ras took a drink of tea, staring into his cup. "My exposure began long ago," he said softly.

"You've been trying to keep the descendants of Lashasn free from the Hjan."

He nodded. "I have tried. I have failed."

"But they're safe now." And studying with the A'ras, with Invar, someone who would be able to help guide them so that they were able to reach as much of their potential as possible. That had been his contribution to the peace and the accords. Ras had agreed, but had done so reluctantly.

"They are safe."

"You don't like it that others watch over them."

"Tell me, Carth of Ih-lash, how do you feel about the fact that your parents left you in Nyaesh?"

"My mother didn't leave me. She was killed—"

"Killed as she attempted to leave you. It is the same, is it not?"

Carth squeezed her eyes shut. Was it the same? She had hated her time on the streets, struggling to find her way, missing her parents and everything she'd known. Had she not chanced upon Jhon… but *had* she? Had it only been chance, especially with what she now knew about her father? It was possible that he had pushed Jhon to find her, and then pushed her to join the A'ras, much as her mother had once wanted. If that was the case, then Carth had been a part of another's game for longer than she'd realized.

"I don't like that I lost her."

"As you should not. Had she lived, I doubt she would have liked leaving you with the A'ras, but as she must have known about your potential with the S'al, she did what she needed to see you trained. It hurts, but that doesn't make it less right."

Carth took her tea and took a drink. The tea was a bitter brew, one that was stronger than what she'd drunk growing up, but contained hints of bayander that filled her nose. She understood what Ras was telling her, and understood the reason that he shared with her.

"Why Odian?" she asked after a while.

"Because it was safe."

Carth looked over at him, starting to smile, but her smile faded when she saw the sadness on his face. "Was?"

"Most sailors know of Odian, which makes it easier for others to reach me. Once here, it is difficult to find."

"You mean that *you* are difficult to find."

"Are they different?"

She shook her head. "The descendants of Lashasn sent their children to you?"

Ras swept his arm behind him, waving toward the doorway. Behind it, Carth knew there were dozens of rooms, though she had not been in any other than the cell where he'd kept her while she was here. "They sent their children to learn. For many years, I taught the descendants of Lashasn, showing them how to use the S'al, allowing them to hold on to that heritage, a piece of history that we would otherwise have lost. Now... now I will not."

"Why did they send them here?"

"The story behind Ih and Lashasn is not one you need me to share."

"That's not what I'm asking. Why here rather than Nyaesh? Why not bolster the A'ras?" she asked.

"In Nyaesh, there were the descendants of Lashasn, but they were those who wanted to maintain the war. Those I was willing to teach were those who had abandoned the belief that the war must continue, who understood that we needed to remain hidden, much as those of Reshian managed to hide in the shadows. While on

Odian, we were able to do that, if only for a while. Those of Ih had their own protection."

"The Reshian."

"The Reshian," Ras agreed.

"They've disappeared. I can't find them."

"Because you haven't searched."

"I have."

"Have you, Carthenne of Ih-lash? Have you visited every possibility? Do you really understand everything that you need to see?"

"Ih-lash is gone."

"Everything changes. We must change as well."

Carth hadn't realized the extent of what had changed. She knew that the Hjan had drawn the Reshian out and had forced them against the A'ras, but had they known the extent of what Ras did?

They must have, to implicate him and to take those of Lashasn as they had.

It was a part of the game she hadn't accounted for.

Yet, somehow, she had still managed to win.

Not win. A truce. There hadn't been another play, so both sides had agreed to peace. That wasn't the same as winning.

How long would the peace hold?

Carth had to believe it wouldn't be nearly as long as she had thought it would.

Ras had raised another concern, one she hadn't considered before now. Could the C'than have used her?

She thought it possible, but less likely. If they were to use her, they would have needed to know what she was capable of doing, and she didn't think that was the case.

Or had they?

Her father was one of the Reshian—and had had Jhon watch over her.

Invar—one of the masters of the A'ras—had worked with her and then sent her with Jhon.

How many others had been the same?

Were they of the C'than?

Was *that* the power Ras implied?

What if Ras worked with the C'than, and only pretended that he didn't?

She looked at him, wondering if perhaps she had been a piece in a game all along. If that was the case, then it was possible that she had missed something, all while thinking she was acting on her own. Maybe she hadn't been. Maybe she *never* had been, always pressed by other pieces, moved as if she were the stone in some massive game of Tsatsun.

The idea actually amused her.

"Why are you smiling?"

"I'm seeing things from a different perspective," she said.

"That often leads to insight."

She nodded. "It does."

"And what did you learn this time?"

Carth took the pieces from the Tsatsun board and arranged them, placing the stone in the middle. "I begin to wonder if you haven't been playing your best."

Ras's eyes sparkled slightly. "You've beaten me three times, Carth of Ih-lash. I think you have won."

Carth leaned forward, thinking through what she'd seen when she'd played him before. Had any of the games been legitimate? Could he have been playing a different game all along?

"I've done what you wanted all along, haven't I?"

Ras folded his arms over his chest. "If that's what you believe…"

"I think you've wanted me to believe I beat you. It's another game for you, isn't it?" She sat back, trying to think through the board. When she saw it this way, when she considered everything she knew, she could piece it together. Now that she did, she began to see how it all came together. Not just the moves, but the individuals she'd worked with ever since losing her mother. Jhon. Invar. Ras. They were all a part of it, weren't they?

They were all a part of a game where *she* had served as the stone.

But why?

"You *are* a part of the C'than, aren't you?"

Ras didn't answer. Instead, he stood, turned to the wall, and disappeared.

CHAPTER 11

CARTH HAD ONLY VAGUE MEMORIES OF HER HOMELAND.

Her parents had left Ih-lash when she was young, taking her from nation to nation and city to city as they had traveled, always searching for something. Now she understood that her parents had searched for safety, and done so in the only way that they had known how. Had they only shared with her while her mother had been alive... would anything have been different?

Ras had disappeared, leaving Carth with the same questions she had before, but also some answers. She needed to find Ih-lash. From there, the Reshian. And then what?

Did she search for the C'than?

Was that what he wanted?

They were two days out from Odian when they found the ship dead in the water.

Guya sailed up to it, his back stiff, making a point of not looking over at her.

"What is it, Guya?" she asked.

"You should stay here."

"Guya?"

"This is a Reshian ship. The shape is too typical for them."

"Where is the crew?"

"I don't know. Stay on the *Spald*."

Carth ignored him and jumped aboard the other ship.

It was strange and empty. There was nothing here. The entire ship was empty. She searched from the helm to the hull and found nothing. The only thing she *did* find were a few scorch marks, but that didn't make any sense to her.

As she stood on the hull, looking up at the furled sails, she frowned. "What happened here, Guya?" Her gaze lingered on the maroon sails, and she wondered why the Reshian chose that color of sail.

"I don't know."

"They're just… gone."

"Aye."

"There were strange burn marks in the hold," Carth said.

Guya's face looked troubled, and Carth realized why the scorch marks had bothered her. They looked almost as if they had been made by the S'al rather than a natural flame. But if that was the case… then the A'ras had violated the accords already.

"I saw them as well."

"They *wanted* the accords," she said.

"Most did."

"Most?" She looked over, waiting for his answer.

"Not all wanted them, Carth. They were used to the fighting, and used to what they knew. You settled it, but will it last?"

"It has to last," Carth said softly.

"That's what you want, but I'm not sure it can."

Guya climbed back onto the *Spald*, saying nothing more. Carth lingered a while longer before following him, and they sailed off, leaving the Reshian ship empty and alone in the middle of the sea.

———

Guya sailed them across the sea, and they came across no other sign of the Reshian, nothing else that seemed out of place. The waves were calm, as if the sea itself sensed her mood and wanted nothing more than to help her reach her homeland and find her answers. Carth didn't think she used her abilities as they sailed, but she had been known to use them without intending to, so it was possible that she had.

"You're quiet," Dara said.

Carth nodded. "I was born here," she said, nodding toward the distant shores. Far in the distance, she could make out the outlines of buildings as they sailed toward the city of Isahl, once the capital of Ih-lash. Was it still? Everything she'd learned from the Reshian, and from Jhon, told her that the Hjan had attacked Ih-lash and had destroyed the city, but buildings remained standing. There would have to be some people still there, though she doubted there would be any with shadow blessings.

"Born but never returned?"

She shook her head. "I think my father knew what was coming. He brought us away, presumably to safety."

Dara laughed softly. "Presumably? You live, Carth. Had they not…"

"Had they not, I might have died. Or they might have died sooner. Or maybe not at all. I don't know."

Dara clutched the railing. "It's a shame you never really had a home. I remember Var, and the home I grew up in—the warmth of the hearth, the laughter of my parents and sister…"

"You could still return."

"And miss all of this?"

Carth forced a smile. "You haven't shared with me *why* you've been willing to come with me. After what we've faced, I keep expecting you to ask to return."

"Does there need to be a why?"

Carth grunted softly. "When your life is constantly in danger, I think there should be a why."

"It's not constantly in danger."

Carth laughed. "Fine. Mostly." She turned to Dara and noted the wrinkles in the corners of her eye as she stared over the bow of the ship, taking in the looming sight of Isahl. Her eyes glistened softly, and tears had formed. "You don't have to risk yourself for this."

"You did. You do."

"I have abilities."

Dara turned to her and flashed a forced smile. "When you rescued us, I thought I was about to die. The fire…"

"That was my fault."

"Even before that, they had been cruel. Hard. There was little doubt that they were going to hurt us. I don't know where they intended to bring us, but they sailed south. They would sell us, and then return and do it again."

"They won't hurt anyone else, Dara."

"They won't, but others like them will. If there aren't those willing to stand up for themselves, and to stand up for others, what's to stop it from happening again? What's to stop worse from happening?"

Carth sighed. Maybe that was the reason she risked herself. Did she do it because others would not?

"I don't want anyone else getting hurt. That includes you."

"Then keep teaching me," she suggested. "I made a mistake on the *Tempar*. It won't happen again."

Carth squeezed her eyes shut. "I don't know."

"Please. Help make me stronger so I can work with you. You can't do this alone, Carth. You're strong—I've seen that much—but everyone needs support. I can be that support."

"I'll think on it."

They sailed the rest of the way into the port of Isahl without another word. Carth didn't remember the city well. She had left Ih-lash when she was quite young, but even then she hadn't spent much time in the capital city. Returning now was out of necessity more than desire, though she recognized that she needed to come back. She needed answers, and she needed to understand herself, before she could really understand what else she might be able to do.

And she needed to find her father. The leader of the Reshian might have answers, not only those she needed to know about the attack and the blood magic, but about herself.

"How will you know where to find what you're looking for?" Dara asked.

That was the one thing she actually *didn't* worry about. With the shadow magic, she'd be able to reach for the changes in the shadows and use them to find others who might be shadow blessed, possibly shadow born, though she wondered if she would find anyone with that ability. There weren't many shadow born—few enough that she doubted any still existed other than her.

"The shadows will guide me."

After anchoring and rowing into the port on a small dinghy, Carth stood in Isahl with Dara. Guya remained on board the ship, ready to depart quickly were there the need.

Carth took a deep breath, inhaling the scents of the city. There was nothing familiar here, nothing that felt like home, not the way the scents and sounds of Nyaesh did. They were at least familiar to her. She had been so long away from Ih-lash that there wasn't anything about the city that *was* familiar. Even the sea had a mossy odor to it that it didn't have farther south.

The sky was overcast, fitting in some ways, letting shadows slide across the ground. Carth maintained a connection to the shadows, but not tightly. She didn't want to reveal her presence too soon, though she needed the connection in order to detect whether there were others with the shadow blessing.

"Where should we go?" Dara asked.

Carth scanned the street running along the harbor. Where in the city *would* she go to find the help she needed? Holding on to nothing more than a streamer of shadow ability, she used that connection to try and detect others with shadow ability, but did not find anything, not while standing on the shore. For her to find what she needed, she would need to go deeper into the city, something she wasn't sure Dara would be willing to do.

"You can return to the *Spald*. I'll go in—"

"You're not going to do this alone. Haven't you shown me enough to keep me safe?"

Carth wasn't sure that she had. If Dara had more time with Ras, she might have learned enough to use the S'al ability—the girl was talented, and maybe more than Carth when it came to that aspect of her ability—but Dara had wanted to come with her. And now Dara had shown an impulsivity that left Carth nervous. What if she attacked again?

"Maybe other places, but here? This is where you will face those who control the shadows," she said.

Dara forced a smile. "You've shown me there is nothing to fear with the shadows, not the way I once did. Besides, you need the help."

It wasn't that she *wanted* to head into Isahl on her own, but she understood that welcoming Dara into the city and bringing her with her created a different set of challenges. She would have to stay near Dara, protect her if things turned sour. And prevent her from doing anything stupid. Within Isahl, there was a possibility that others might be able to counter her ability with shadows.

But since she didn't know what she might encounter, having another with Lashasn abilities would help, and might keep her safer.

A door to the nearest building opened, and a young man with a pale face stepped out. He eyed Carth and then Dara for a long moment before stepping back into the building and closing the door.

Dara tensed but didn't make any other movement.

"I need the help," Carth finally agreed.

They started into the city, simply walking the streets. Carth didn't know what she searched for, more of a sense against her, a presence that would help her know that others who could control the shadows existed. What would she do when she found them? She hadn't worked that out yet, other than knowing she needed answers. If anyone would have them, it would be someone in Ih-lash, wouldn't it?

"How do you intend to find your father?" Dara asked in a whisper.

Carth glanced at her. Dara was intuitive, and though she hadn't said anything about what she intended with finding her father, Dara still had known. She shouldn't have expected anything else.

"I don't know," she said.

"You haven't said anything about him since we left Wesjan. I thought you might want to search for him before now."

"I have."

"Not really. We've sailed to different ports, but you haven't really attempted to find the Reshian before now."

"What would I say?"

"What do you intend to say now?"

Carth shook her head. She didn't know what she would say, but there would be questions asked. They had been running through her mind since she had first seen her father alive, and many of them she hadn't had the time to get answers to, but now that she was no longer searching for a way to keep her friends safe, and no longer chasing after the Hjan, she *did* have the time.

But those weren't the questions she wanted answered.

She needed to know about the Reshian, and she needed to know about the attacks she'd seen. What was the blood magic? She knew it wasn't the Hjan, but the Hjan *were* interested in what had happened.

As she turned a corner and saw a small square that brought back memories of her mother's death in Nyaesh, she felt a flicker of shadows moving.

The sense was indistinct, but definitely there.

Carth paused and Dara glanced over to her.

In the darkness, she noted the soft glow to Dara's skin, the sign that she used her S'al ability. Carth shook her head at Dara. "You shouldn't—"

She didn't get the chance to finish warning Dara to release the light.

Shadows surged around them, thick like a sudden fog, and Dara cried out.

Carth remained motionless.

The shadows didn't affect her, but they *did* cut her off from her connection to the S'al, even augmented as it was by the ring she wore. More than that, by overpowering the shadows, whoever attacked was able to take that ability away from her as well. It was the same thing Ras had done, using the S'al against her, using his connection to the flame to steal away the heat, and the light to push back the shadows.

Dara looked over to her, panic flashing in her eyes, but Carth shook her head slightly. "Wait," she mouthed, uncertain whether Dara could even see through the darkness. Carth could, but that was more because she was tied to the shadows.

The other girl slid toward Carth, holding her hand near the knife she carried. If she unsheathed it, Carth suspected the shadows would constrict even more.

They had to wait.

She didn't know what they waited for.

Not more of an attack. This would likely be all they experienced. The shadows were dense, but likely only to prevent them from escaping.

The longer she stood, the easier it was for her to sense the depths of the shadows. As she did, she could feel the power swirling within it. This power had both a direction and a source.

Taking a deep breath, she swept her hand around her, drawing the shadows toward her, and then up, lifting them from the street.

There was resistance. With the shadows, she had rarely felt any such resistance. She either had the connection, or she did not. Bright sunlight could obscure them from her, as could someone like Ras, powerful with the S'al, the A'ras flame. This was something different—

someone with the strength of the shadows, and given the way they were used, possibly shadow born.

But Carth was stronger.

She detected that as she pressed upon the tendrils of darkness, raising them from the street, tearing them free from where they attempted to hold both her and Dara.

With one final surge of strength, Carth forced them completely away.

The street was clear. There were only her and Dara, standing alone.

Carth clasped her hands behind her back. Whoever attacked would come again. And she would wait.

CHAPTER 12

CARTH NOTED THE WAY DARA SHIFTED HER STANCE FROM foot to foot, her gaze darting around the buildings, as if she could determine the source of the attack. There was no source identifiable, just as there was no attack right now. They had to wait.

"Where are they?" Dara whispered.

Carth motioned toward the building nearest them. She could detect the pull of the shadows strongest from there, but nothing else.

"What are we doing?" Dara asked.

"Waiting." Was this why Ras had suggested she return to her homeland? Had he known she needed to find this?

"For what?"

The shadows built again, but this time it was a subtle sensation, barely more than a pulse against her senses. Carth pulled on the shadows, folding them around her, as she allowed the user of the shadows to realize that she was here.

"For that."

The door to a building down the street opened and a dark-haired man with eyes that blazed a deep brown—nearly black—exited. Shadows swirled around his feet, tracing down his long leather overcoat, trailing along the street. Carth had never seen anyone like him.

When she had studied with the A'ras, she'd considered Samis attractive. He had the traditional brown hair and muscular frame that so many within Nyaesh possessed, but it was his intelligence and compassion that had always drawn her to him, even when it should not have. This man made Samis look plain.

Was it the shadows that pulled her toward him, or was it something else, a more primal connection, one forged by the shadows and her connection to the people of Ih-lash?

Dara grabbed at her arm and held her in place.

Carth took a deep breath, shaking away the fog that had fallen over her mind.

How could some man have such an effect on her?

"I know he's pretty, but stay by me?" Dara suggested.

Carth nodded, trying to keep her face neutral as the man approached.

"You are shadow born," he said. Even his voice had a deep timbre, one that matched his dress and the way the shadows swirled around him.

"Who are you?"

The man offered a half-smile. "You come into Isahl and question me?"

"You attacked me. I think I have every right to question."

The man shook his head. "Not you." He motioned to Dara. "We attacked her. We've been assaulted often enough by Lashasn to recognize them."

Carth kept Dara close. If they thought to attack her again, she might need to use her control of the shadows on him again. She'd discovered that she was stronger than him—at least she thought she was—so she hoped that if it came to that, she would be able to ensure Dara got to safety. She didn't want it to come to an attack, though. She had come for answers.

"Are you Reshian?" Carth asked.

The man's eyes narrowed. "What do you know of the Reshian?"

Carth shrugged, hoping it appeared casual. She realized that she might have been too trusting coming into Isahl. She didn't know anything about the city, and had come thinking that her ability with the shadows would have her welcomed, but she should have planned for the possibility that they would have been displeased with her coming.

"I know of many things. I have seen the Reshian. I have known the A'ras. I know there is a peace accord now, one that should bring a lasting—"

He turned away from her, the shadows swirling around him.

Carth wasn't accustomed to others turning their backs on her like this man. She had already proven what she was capable of doing, but it didn't seem to matter to him.

Carth stretched the shadows toward him, but he waved them off.

The way that he did proved that he was stronger than he'd let on during the first attack.

Maybe she was wrong. Maybe he was stronger than her. If that was the case, she needed to be more cautious.

Carth followed him toward the building.

Dara clung to her arm, squeezing tightly. If she could, Carth would have preferred to send Dara back to the ship to wait for her. She needed to know what was going on here, and why this man seemed annoyed by her referencing the accords.

When they reached the door inside the building, she hesitated.

The shadows were deeper here. As she reached for them, she had a sense that they wouldn't respond as well to her as they did to the man. Did the shadows care who used them?

More than information, she had another reason for wanting to follow him. If he was shadow born like her, what could she learn? She had none to teach her how to use that skill of hers, and had fumbled along, trying to do what she could with it, discovering the extent of her abilities as best as she could. But learning from someone else would be easier, and she might discover a way to use the shadows in ways she hadn't considered. Maybe he would have answers about the blood magic, and why the shadows had failed her then.

"Are you sure we should do this?" Dara asked.

Carth wasn't, but they weren't going to get anywhere by remaining cautious. She wasn't going to learn what she wanted being cautious. The man could use the shadows, and she hoped he could lead her to the Reshian—and her father.

She stepped into the shadowed room.

As she did, the darkness retreated. It was as if it needed to stay away from her.

Not her, she realized. The darkness retreated from Dara.

"I don't think I'm supposed to be here," Dara whispered.

"Because you're not supposed to be here."

The shadow-born man stepped toward her. His arms were crossed, and Carth noted a knife strapped to his belt, one that reminded her of the one she now possessed from her father. He didn't unsheathe it. If he did, Carth would do what she had to in order to protect Dara.

It wasn't that she was completely dependent on her magic, either. She had trained with the A'ras, which made her skilled with both the sword and the knife. Those skills had saved her before, such as when she had faced the man on the ship while rescuing Dara and the others who had been captured with her.

If it came to needing to attack, Carth would be ready.

She watched the man, studying him as he approached. The shadows seemed possessive of him, swirling around him in such a way that Carth doubted she would be able to separate them from him were she to need to escape.

"Why have you come here?" he asked.

"This is Ih-lash. I didn't realize that I needed to answer for why I would come."

He shot Carth a hard look, which she matched. "I didn't speak to you. Her," he said, jabbing his thumb toward Dara. "Why have you come? Your place is in the south. That was the agreement. Do you think to violate it again?"

"That wasn't the agreement." Carth didn't know every-thing about the differences between Ih and Lashasn, but she understood the accords.

The man sneered at her, the expression soiling his otherwise lovely face. "You have come to Ih and you think you know all that we have been through?"

"Ih? Not Ih-lash?"

He waved his hand and the shadows started to thin. "Ih-lash is no more. Now we are only Ih."

"What of Lashasn?" Carth asked.

"Those lands were destroyed by the invaders."

Carth glanced over to Dara, wishing that she had someone else with her who might know more than she did about what they were encountering. Everyone she'd spoken to had told her how Ih-lash was no more. They had said nothing about how it was now only Ih once more.

"What attack?"

"The one her kind instigated."

"Her kind. We were once a single people," Carth said.

The man turned his attention to her. In the darkness and shadows, Carth could still tell the way his eyes blazed, anger and a touch of hatred burning within them. "We? You are not of Ih."

"I was born of Ih-lash." Carth made a point of pulling on the shadows, wanting to draw his attention. There was nothing else she could be other than of Ih-lash.

The man stood, arms crossed, disinterested. "You

might have been born in Ih-lash, and you might be shadow touched, but you are not *of* Ih-lash. If you were, you would never travel with one like her."

Carth wondered what had happened. The last she had heard, there had been peace in Ih-lash. The Reshian might have fought against the A'ras, but that was part of an older war, one that was separate from Ih-lash.

And she had thought that the accords had brought peace. That they would have settled the ancient conflict. They had not.

"It was a mistake coming here," she said to Dara, turning her so they could leave.

When she turned, she saw two others blocking her way. Both were younger, one a girl who couldn't have been much older than Dara, and the other a young man with long hair hanging over his eyes. Though both watched her, creating a physical barricade that wasn't the reason she paused. It was the way the shadows swirled around them, practically clinging to them the same as they did with the other man. There didn't seem the same level of control as what she'd seen from the man, which made her suspect they were shadow blessed only.

Carth wondered if she could manage something like what they did. When the other man had approached them in the street, the shadows had remained around him, as if providing protection. When she'd first discovered her shadow ability, Jhon had taught her how to sink into the shadows, and how to use them to cloak herself. That was when he'd thought she was only shadow blessed. Having the shadows linger would give her an advantage, and would allow her to have them accessible at all times.

She tried pulling on the shadows, using a subtle touch, but they didn't move. The shadows didn't respond to her, as if these shadow blessed had used them to cloak themselves, or had claimed the shadows in some way.

She frowned.

The two watching her blocked her from leaving, but Carth stepped forward. "Move," she said.

The woman looked past Carth to the other man.

"If you don't move, you'll learn what *I* can do with the shadows," she said.

This time, Carth didn't use the same subtle touch. She pulled, drawing with all the strength she possessed, tearing the shadows free from the other two. The shadows might be attuned to them, but she was shadow born.

The woman gasped, but it was the younger of the two Carth focused her attention upon. As she watched, he *faded*.

There was no other way to describe what he did.

He was there, and then he was not.

Carth pulled the shadows away, tearing them free from both the man and the woman, but she still saw no sign of him. Spinning, she noted the other man was gone as well.

What had happened? How had they disappeared on her so quickly?

"Where did they go?" Dara asked.

Carth used the shadows, pulling on them as she tried to determine where the two men had gone, but detected nothing.

The girl tried sinking into the shadows. Carth noted it

as a shifting of them, as if she intended to sag into them, cloaking herself. She'd worked with the shadows enough that she recognized what the girl did, and resisted.

Turning to her, Carth stared.

"Where did they go?"

The girl shook her head.

"I won't ask again. Where did they go?"

"You won't find them. Andin would have taken them both to safety."

"Andin is the shadow born?"

The girl's eyes widened. "You knew?"

"How do you think I'm stopping you from cloaking yourself?"

The girl nodded to Dara. "She's with you."

Dara had a soft glow to her now that the others had departed, just enough to push back the shadows a little, but not enough to make it clear that she used the power of the S'al. It wouldn't defeat a shadow born, and it wouldn't have been enough to stop even a shadow blessed from sinking too deeply into the shadows.

"She's with me," Carth said. "That doesn't mean she's attacking you."

"Then how…" Her eyes widened again. "You really are shadow born?"

Carth decided not to answer. "Bring her with us," she said to Dara.

"Where?"

"Back to the ship. We need answers, and now we've got someone we can ask." If nothing else, she would sail them back to Odian and force Ras to provide answers.

The girl's eyes stayed wide as Dara motioned for her to leave the building.

Carth looked around before departing. She had come back to Ih-lash thinking that she would find information about her home, and maybe something about where she'd come from, but all she had discovered were more questions. This time, she didn't even think the Hjan were involved. In some ways, that made it worse.

CHAPTER 13

"Tell me again," Carth said, sitting across from the young woman, whose name she'd learned was Lindy. She had dark hair and pale skin that was typical for Ih. Carth had bound her wrists, choosing reluctantly to do so when the girl had continued to fight while they'd made the crossing to the *Goth Spald*. Had she not restrained her, the girl would have kicked so much she'd have ended up falling off the dinghy.

"I've answered your questions already." Lindy thrust her chin out but didn't look at Carth. Her focus was on Dara.

Every so often, Carth would feel the shifting of shadows and knew that Lindy attempted to pull on them again. Each time she did so, Carth resisted, settling them back to her, forcing them away from Lindy. She doubted the girl would be able to do much more than obscure herself slightly, but she didn't know with certainty whether she would be able to do anything more.

"You've told me you served Andin."

"You don't understand. You're not—"

"Of Ih, I understand that completely," Carth said, shaking her head. Lindy had made that point over and again. Each time she did, Carth made a point of telling her how she was born of Ih-lash, but brought away at a young age. It didn't seem to matter to Lindy. Remaining was the only thing that mattered. "Then tell me about the Reshian."

She needed to understand why Andin had seemed angered when she had mentioned the Reshian. She had thought they were the descendants of Ih, but then she had also thought the A'ras were the descendants of Lashasn, and that wasn't the case, at least not entirely. Was there a more complicated answer with the Reshian?

When Lindy didn't answer, Carth let out a long sigh. "I'm just trying to understand. You're clearly prepared for an attack," she said. That had to be the reason Andin had so quickly found her. And if they'd found her once, she suspected they would again, though she would be better prepared for whatever they might attempt.

"It wouldn't be the first time."

"The first time for what?"

She nodded to Dara. "That *her* kind attacked us here. There have been more lately."

"And the Reshian?"

Lindy shook her head. "They abandoned us. They were supposed to be the defenders of Ih, but they abandoned us."

The door opened and Guya filled the door frame. His

gaze darted from Carth to Dara and then to Lindy. "You should release her," he said.

"We haven't done anything to her, Guya," Carth said, keeping her gaze on Lindy.

"Not yet, but they might do something to us."

"What do you mean?"

"Come."

Carth glanced to Dara. "Watch her."

Dara nodded. Carth worried a little about anything happening between Lindy and Dara, but prayed that Dara was too smart to let herself get pulled into an attack. Maybe using Dara might intimidate Lindy a little more, at least enough to encourage her to speak.

Back on the deck, Guya led her to the bow and pointed. "What do you see there?"

Carth stared where he pointed, back into the city. Running along the shore, a thick blanket of dark fog began to swirl, filling the streets and stretching toward the ship.

"Ever see fog like that?" he asked.

"That's not fog," she said softly.

"Didn't think so. What did you find in the Isahl?"

"Someone like me."

"Why would they attack?"

Carth watched the shadows slowly start to ooze across the bay. Much longer and they would reach the ship. The control was impressive. If this was from Andin, she needed to find him again, if only to learn from him. How much could she discover of her abilities from someone who actually knew how to use them?

"I thought the Hjan responsible for what happened to Ih-lash," she said.

"They were attacked. Rumors out of here were that the cities were destroyed. I never knew if it was the Hjan or something else," Guya said. "What are you going to do now?"

She would have to decide whether to fight or to run. She could use the shadows to help propel the ship, but it wasn't something she could rely upon against another shadow born. Had she the same ability as the Hjan, she could simply flicker from place to place. She had to admit, traveling like that would have advantages.

She glanced toward the stairs leading into the belly of the *Spald*. She could hold on to Lindy and get answers from her, but was that the way she wanted to do it?

Besides, was that even the right move?

It had been a while since she'd thought about her actions in terms of Tsatsun, but it still applied. Everything she'd learned from Ras had value, especially as she worked to discover why Ih and Lashasn fought once more. If it was because of the Hjan, then the accords should have solved it, but if there was something else, she needed to understand so she would know how to position herself.

"Watch them," she said to Guya.

He grunted. "Are you sure this is what you should do? Is this your move?"

She smiled. They'd played Tsatsun a few times while traveling together. Guya had a mind for it, but wasn't at her level. Eventually, she thought he could be quite skilled. "I don't know what the right move is. I need more information. Then I'll decide."

"Don't sacrifice the wrong piece."

"I'll keep you safe."

"That's not the piece I was concerned about," he told her.

Carth smiled, pulling on the shadows, already beginning to feel some resistance from the shadows on the edge of the bay. "I'll be fine, too."

She wrapped herself in darkness.

As she did, she jumped.

Holding on to the shadows in this way gave her the advantage of strength, which she used now, and the ability to turn the shadows into something real, almost physical. With her connection to them, she was able to draw upon the shadows, pull them to her, and slide along them like they were solid.

She reached the shore faster than were she to take the dinghy.

As she did, she pressed out, drawing upon the S'al through the ring she'd taken from her mother. Using this, she was able to disperse the fog, and it shattered in front of her.

Carth stood on the shore, looking for Andin.

He would be here somewhere.

"I know you're here, Andin," Carth called. She used the shadows to amplify her voice, the same way she often had used them to mute her passing.

A moment passed, and he emerged from between a pair of buildings. As before, shadows swirled around him.

There was no effort to hide the rage on his face. "You're one of them."

"I am Carthenne Rel of Ih-lash," she said.

"Am I supposed to be impressed?"

Carth stepped toward him. "I am descended from both Ih and Lashasn. Think of that what you will."

Andin pushed on the shadows, but using the power of the S'al, Carth was able to resist. She held on to this connection, maintaining it as she approached him. With it, she added her connection to the shadows, holding both. There was always more power for her when she used both, and this time was no different. When she did, she was able to detect the edge of the shadows as well as form them. While holding both, she could press upon the light, drawing heat and fire from within her, the flame she had learned to use while in the A'ras.

Magic poured from her.

"Are you here to conquer?" Andin asked. "You will find we do not fall easily. Others have tried and failed. You might be powerful, Carthenne Rel of Ih-lash, but you are still only one person."

Carth took a deep breath and released most of her hold on her powers.

The shadows snapped back into place, essentially consuming Andin. She stood, connected to only a thread of her powers, wanting to demonstrate that she had no intent to harm them.

"I am not here to conquer."

Andin stepped forward, shedding the shadows around him as he did. They pooled at his feet, leaving him standing with enough power that she suspected he could attack her quickly. It was possible what he held would be enough for him to disappear, much the same way the other man had disappeared. That was a trick she wanted to learn. Then again, she would like to learn how Andin managed to generate a fog. She had power but no control, nothing like what she had seen.

"Why have you come, Carthenne Rel?"

What answer would satisfy him? What could she tell him that would make it so he didn't think she wanted to attack him? She suspected he would always question her. His posture made it clear that he doubted what she might say, and his hand hovering near the knife made her wary that he might still attack. She had proven herself strong— a credible threat—and that might make him dangerous.

But if she opposed him, and if she made it clear that she would fight back, she wouldn't learn what she wanted. She needed to understand the Reshian. She needed to find her father. She needed to learn more about the attacks. And she needed to understand the shadows. If she didn't, would she ever understand herself?

"I came to know the place of my birth. I intended to come home."

Andin watched her for a moment with an unreadable expression. Carth half-expected him to reach for the shadows again, and to unsheathe his knife and attack. If he did, she would have no choice but to fight back, but she didn't want to do so. Andin was shadow born. And though she had met others with her ability with the A'ras magic, she had never yet met anyone else with the same ability with the shadows.

"Ih-lash is no more, Carthenne Rel."

"Then help me understand what happened."

He glanced past her, his gaze traveling out to the ship before he turned his attention back to Carth. "If you release my sister, I will share what I can."

Carth nodded. "Lindy will be released."

Andin nodded. "Then we can talk."

CHAPTER 14

ANDIN LED CARTH AND LINDY TO THE SAME BUILDING
where she had found him the first time. She'd asked Dara
to remain on the ship, not wanting to force another
confrontation, and Dara had grudgingly agreed. Lindy
had gone with Carth willingly, though she had been
quieter than when she was first captured. Had Dara said
anything to her to quiet her? She almost expected it from
Dara—especially with how she had behaved on the
Tempar—but hoped that she could trust Dara to restrain
herself.

"Why here?" Carth asked as the door closed
behind them.

Andin used the shadows in a way that Carth hadn't
considered, sealing them around the walls and filling the
cracks, practically enclosing them in the room together so
nothing would escape.

She still held on to the connection to the shadows and
held a trickle of the S'al as well, just enough to keep

herself focused. With that connection, she was able to feel the edge of the shadows. It was the same as Jhon had instructed her long ago, the guidance enough for her to gain more than a passing understanding of how to sink into the shadows, and how to cloak herself with them.

"Here is where we're the safest," he said. He stood with his back to the far wall, and Lindy stood next to him, her hands stuffed into her pockets. She looked at the floor rather than meeting Carth's eyes. Andin stared defiantly at her.

It was then Carth recognized the pull on the shadows.

It was subtle, no less so than what she had experienced before, and this pull tugged enough, a sagging within the shadows, that she suspected it came from someone who was shadow blessed.

With the way that she felt the shadows, she suspected it was more than one person here who was shadow blessed.

Lindy didn't use them, she didn't think, but there had been the other boy she'd seen. He was barely old enough to have been considered a man. Were there others like him?

Carth turned slowly, probing gently with the S'al power rather than using the shadows. Here, with whatever it was that Andin was able to do with the shadows, she doubted she would be able to control them with as much delicacy as would be needed.

As she probed, she noted at least three other shadow blessed.

Carth tipped her head. There was something off about all of this, but she couldn't quite place it. Andin watched her, and she wondered what he saw. Did he notice a soft glowing, the same way that she noticed it around Dara when she pulled on the connection to the S'al? Did he see nothing? With the power she'd detected from him, Carth doubted it was nothing. He would have picked up on something from her.

As she looked at them, she realized what it was that bothered her.

They were all young.

Andin couldn't have been but a year or two older than her. Lindy was younger, at least five years younger than Carth, and Andin had claimed her as his sister. The other boy she'd seen was young as well. Were the others hiding in shadows equally young?

Her mind raced through what she'd seen.

The city was essentially empty. It had to be for them to move openly and use their abilities like they did. There had been the attack, presumably from the Hjan—or from Lashasn, as they claimed. There was a small group of shadow blessed and a single shadow born. There was no one else.

And the Reshian had left them.

That seemed the strangest to her.

If she knew anything about the Reshian, it was that they had prized the connection they shared, the bond to the shadows. They wouldn't have left others with the same ability behind in Isahl, not when they would be able to use them.

There was something she missed, but what was it?

In her mind, she formed the parts of a Tsatsun board,

and arranged the pieces as she knew. She still didn't have an answer.

"How long have you been here alone?" she asked.

Andin frowned. "We're not alone."

The confidence she'd seen from him at first took on a different meaning. What she had assumed to be bravado, and a kind of arrogance about his abilities, might be something else.

She tipped her head, seeing him—really seeing him—for the first time.

"How old are you?" she asked.

Andin pulled on the shadows. As he did, she realized *why*. The effect gave him a sense of age that he didn't have otherwise.

She focused her attention on the shadows at his feet, the ones that pooled around him. With those, she used the gentlest of touches with the S'al, sending them skittering away. She wondered if he would even be aware of what she did. Likely, especially given the strength she'd seen he possessed, but she risked it to know.

The shadows slowly separated from him.

For the first time, she realized that the appearance he'd worn had been something other than what she'd expected, almost as if he had used the shadows to create lines in his face that weren't there, and add age that he had not yet earned. A glamour, and one of incredible skill.

He couldn't even be her age.

They were all young. Which would likely be why the shadows remained near them. They had figured out a way to make themselves seem older. She could think of many reasons for them to do it, but only a few that made any real sense.

"You're the only ones in the city, aren't you?" she asked.

Lindy looked over to Andin, her eyes wide. They hadn't expected her to work it out, or they hadn't expected her to discover it.

Andin's face contorted, twisting in a mask of anger. "You're in Isahl. There is an entire city—"

Carth took a step toward him. She pulsed on the shadows, sending a pulse of the S'al power as well. Combining them like that, she was able to sense the neighboring buildings. There was nothing. They were empty.

That might mean nothing, but then, it could mean everything, especially if the city was truly empty.

"Why are you here alone?"

"We're not alone—"

Carth pulsed on the shadows and the S'al again, this time with more force. It dispersed the effect of what his shadow-born magic did, leaving them standing face-to-face, neither holding much in the way of power.

This close, she noted that he was still pretty, but there had been something about the shadow glamour that had made him even more so. His eyes betrayed the fear he felt, and his hand darting to his knife betrayed his nerves.

"You're afraid of what I might do to you?"

Andin glared at her. The anger he'd displayed when she'd first appeared had returned in full force. It was almost enough to make her laugh, if it weren't for the fact that it was sad that he felt the need to be so independent.

"You aren't the first person to come to Isahl and try to claim those of us who are left."

"I'm not trying to claim you."

"You come to our shores, and you speak of the Reshian, and you bring a child of Lashasn with you. And then you demonstrate powers that should not have been combined. What are we supposed to think but that you would do harm to us?"

Could she really blame them for that reaction? They must have experienced some horror for them to hide and then attack the way they had. When Carth had appeared with the ability to use the shadows, they must have believed that she was like them. Which meant they weren't really afraid of those with shadow abilities.

"What happened to the Reshian? Why haven't you gone with them?"

"The Reshian," Andin spat. "They abandoned us as we said."

"Tell me how."

Lindy nodded to Andin, as if encouraging him to share. "Even after everything else fell, the city was attacked. The attackers grabbed us, pulled us away. We managed to escape, but when we did, the city had been abandoned."

Carth thought about the way the Hjan had attempted collecting in Nyaesh. This sounded far too similar to be chance.

"What did they look like?"

Andin frowned. "They were all different. They were strong. Not just with their bodies, but they had abilities as well. Magic. There wasn't anything we could do to get away."

That also sounded like the Hjan.

"Did they have scars?" she asked, running her hand along the side of her face.

Lindy looked to Andin. "The first attackers did."

"The first?"

"When we returned, the attack was different."

Carth sighed. "Those with the scars are called the Hjan. They are the reason Isahl fell."

Andin shook his head. "Isahl fell because the others abandoned it. The city held after those first attacks, but those who knew the shadows left, abandoning us. They let Lashasn attack us after everyone else was gone."

That wouldn't make sense, but wasn't that what her parents had done? They had ushered her out of the city, wanting to get her away before any attack came. And had they not, they might have been caught in the midst of the Hjan attack.

Had things been different, she might have been here with Andin and Lindy and the others, and she might be the one cowering while strangers appeared with powers that she didn't understand.

"How did you escape?"

No one answered.

Carth frowned. "I've faced the Hjan, and I know how formidable they are. How would you have gotten away? You must have been barely ten years old!"

It was probably younger than that. Carth had been five when they had left Ih-lash, so she suspected they would have been much the same age. That the Hjan would have gone after them at that age… it meant something more coordinated than she had realized. They would have wanted to use them, but in a different way than they would have wanted to use the girls they'd claimed from Odian.

Could they have thought to turn them? Perhaps they'd intended to train them, to make them into Hjan with powers of the shadows as well. That would make for a formidable foe.

"How did you escape?" she asked more gently.

"It was Andin," Lindy offered.

Andin's face reddened. Had he been holding the shadows as he had been before, she doubted that she would have seen it. As it was, she barely noticed the slight shade, a hint of color to his cheeks, enough for her to know that he was embarrassed.

"That was when you discovered you were shadow born, wasn't it?" she asked.

He swallowed and licked his lips before nodding. "I didn't mean to. I tried to stab one of them in the leg so that he couldn't run after us when we got away, but it started to rot. At least, that was what I thought at the time."

Carth smiled grimly. It was hard to feel bad for what had happened to the Hjan, but she understood the feelings Andin must have had after it happened. They were many of the same feelings she'd had after she'd killed Felyn. There was relief, but there was also a sense of regret. A part of her had changed when she had killed. The Nyaesh training had taken other hesitation away from her, but that first one lingered.

"Mine was similar," she started. Carth closed her eyes, the details of that night coming to her so clearly. "I had followed the man who had killed my mother. He was powerful, but I didn't care. I had learned I was shadow blessed and thought I could hide if I needed to. When he attacked, I stabbed him with my father's knife. Darkness poured out of me, and it filled him, going up his arm and into his chest." She opened her eyes. "The shadows might have been the reason he died that night, but it was my hand that killed." She took a deep breath. "I know that if I hadn't done anything, I would have been the one to die that night. And I know that he deserved to die. He had killed others, and I suspect he had been to Ih-lash as well, leading part of the attack here. I don't regret needing to kill him."

Andin's face clouded. "I don't regret killing the man I did either."

There was more anger in him than she had realized at first. It filled him, clouding his words, almost casting shadows on him of a different sort.

Rather than pushing him on it, Carth decided to change the topic. "What happened when you escaped?"

"We came back to the city," Andin said.

"That's it?"

Lindy looked to her brother before answering. "For a while. There weren't many who remained, but there were enough. Then we were attacked again. This time…"

Andin's face hardened. "This time it was Lashasn."

"When was this?" Carth asked.

"A few months ago."

"They wouldn't have attacked. They had agreed to the accords."

Andin shook his head. "I don't know anything about any accords, but they attacked. There was fire and pain, and their ships…"

Carth stared at them and realized they truly believed the Lashasn had attacked.

Could they have?

Would Lashasn have attacked? It would have been after the accords, so it would have violated them. But she didn't think that was likely. It couldn't be.

"What happened then?" Carth asked.

"We hid, at least those of us who could," Lindy said. "Not all could, and when the attacks were over…"

"What?" Carth pressed.

"We found the city empty," Lindy said. She had stepped forward as Carth had shared what she had done with Felyn. "We looked for others that we knew, anyone, but we were alone. Weeks later a ship came in, and they used the shadows. They called themselves the Reshian, and they offered to bring us to others with shadow ability."

"The Reshian are the remnants of Ih-lash," Carth said. "They would have helped you. Until the accords, they still fought on behalf of Ih-lash."

"They didn't want to fight on our behalf," Lindy said. "They left us to Lashasn."

"The Reshian would have done everything they could to help you," Carth told them. "Especially if they had learned that there was a shadow born among you."

Lindy shook her head. "I overheard them. They were talking to someone about us. They would have offered us to the same ones who attacked the city. We stayed hidden."

Could the Reshian have betrayed their own people to the Hjan?

She thought of everything she had known about them, which wasn't much, but the Reshian had fought against the Hjan with the most vigor. For them to have someone who might have betrayed them troubled her.

"What did you hear?"

Lindy started to answer, but Andin set his hand on her arm. "It doesn't matter, Lindy. None of it was real. It couldn't have been."

"Why?" Carth asked.

Andin looked from his sister to Carth. "Because she claims to have heard them talking about putting someone on the ship into…" He looked to his sister for help.

"The see-than," Lindy said.

Carth's breath caught. "That's what you heard? They intended to place someone into the C'than?"

"You've heard of it?" Andin asked.

Carth nodded. "I have now." Could there be some connection?

Lindy nudged him. "See? That *is* what I heard."

"I never said it wasn't, only that I didn't think it was a word."

Without meaning to, she started pressing on the shadows and began gathering the strength of the S'al to her.

"Carthenne Rel?" Lindy said.

Carth opened her eyes and released the power she held.

"What is it?"

"A move I hadn't considered," Carth said. "One that I need to understand, but more than that, it's one *you* need to understand."

"And that is?"

"You need to join the Reshian."

Andin glared at her and shook his head. "You don't understand. The Reshian *abandoned* us."

"They wouldn't have done that, not the Reshian that I've met. They want to work with those with shadow gifts."

"What do you know of the Reshian?" Andin asked.

"I know that I seek them for answers."

"What kind of answers?" Lindy asked.

"The kind only the Reshian can bring."

"Why?" Lindy asked. Shadows swirled around her, the cloak she formed thick with them.

"Because my father now leads them."

CHAPTER 15

The *Goth Spald* was a quick ship, but even a fleet ship could be caught.

They sailed over the sea, making their way west. That was where the children of Isahl claimed they'd seen Reshian sailing. It had been months, so it might be too late for them to find the Reshian, but it was more than Carth had found in her travels so far.

There was a hushed sort of somberness that hung over everything. Even Dara didn't speak, though Carth wondered whether this was because of the presence of the shadow blessed or whether there was something else to it. Of those they had claimed from Isahl, Andin remained mostly quiet. Carth wanted to go to him, thinking she might be able to learn something from him, and have the opportunity to work with another of the shadow born. He stayed away from her, avoiding every attempt she made to go to him, seemingly wanting nothing to do with her.

Lindy was more open. She caught Carth on the deck

of the ship one evening as they were sailing towards Nyaesh. Carth stood at the railing, watching the sea as she so often did, thoughts racing through her mind. Was this something her father would have seen? Had he sailed these waters, going with the others of the Reshian? A part of her wondered if she would ever find him again. She had thought—hoped might be more accurate—that she would find him by going to Ih-lash, but those lands were abandoned. Empty.

When they had traveled away from Ih-lash as a child, they had gone over ground. They had avoided the sea, almost as if it were intentional. Now that she knew her father led the Reshian, she wondered whether he had hidden from them, or whether he had hidden them from it.

Now, she needed to find the Reshian, if only to understand. That had to be the reason Ras had sent her to Isahl —wasn't it?

More and more, she still felt as if she had been used, but now she was no longer certain that mattered. She knew enough that getting used like *this* wasn't the problem. She *wanted* to know what had happened here. She wanted to understand why Isahl thought Lashasn had attacked, or why the Reshian had seemingly abandoned them.

They were answers she was determined to get.

"What do you see when you look out?" Lindy asked.

Garth glanced over to her, ocean spray moistening her face. She wiped it away from her cheek. "Nothing but the sea."

"I never expected to sail it myself," Lindy said. She

focused her gaze outward, staring into the growing darkness. "When I was a child, my mother used to talk about coming across the sea. She romanticized it in many ways. This is nothing like what I expected."

Carth looked over, frowning. "Why would your mother have come across the sea?"

Lindy sighed. "Even in Isahl, we weren't all from there. There were many immigrants. Those of us who came from there often struggled."

"It was the same for me. When my parents left Ih-lash, we stopped in dozens of cities, most only for short stays. Nyaesh was place I remained the longest."

"Then I imagine it was the same for you as it was for my mother."

"We were in Nyaesh for several months before my parents were killed. My mother, at least," she corrected. "My father survived, though I didn't know it at the time. I didn't know much about the city, I didn't know much about the people. I was scared. Was that what it was like for you in Isahl?"

"For me, I was born and raised there. My mother talked about how it was difficult for her coming across the sea, although she did it when she was very young and didn't remember those days. They settled in Isahl and she never moved again. She met my father when she was eighteen and they were married two years later. They had a good life. My father ran a carpenter shop, making furniture and other beautiful items out of ash and oak."

She stopped, a smile spreading across her face. Carth imagined she thought of things her father had made, envisioning what it would have been like.

"Sometimes he was hired for better jobs. He took all who offered, never really caring. He loved the work. I remember him telling me often how much he loved the smell of sawdust, and that of the oils they used, what he called the cleanliness of the shop."

"What of your mother?" Carth asked. She'd never known what her father had done before leaving for Nyaesh, but her mother had cared as much about herbs as about anything else. She must have had an ability with the S'al to have passed it on to Carth, but Carth had never suspected her of using it.

"My mother was a cook and served in one of the local taverns. She rose to head cook and took as much pride in that as if she owned the place."

Lindy fell silent and they stood side by side. Carth listened to the sound of the waves against the hull, and the sound of the groaning of the wood as it carried them through the sea. What did Lindy listen to?

"A woman named Vera was the one who took me in," Carth said, breaking the silence. "I worked in the tavern, collecting scraps and cleaning up after customers left." She smiled to herself. At the time, that had seemed like the worst work she could do, but now… now a part of her longed for the ease of such tasks. It had been a simpler time, one when she had known only the stress of finding coin and sleeping. She sighed before going on. "I still think about her cooking. There's something different about tavern cooking than the cooking anywhere else."

Lindy laughed. "My mother wouldn't cook for us the same way as she would for the tavern. She said there was no need. Occasionally Andin and I would sneak into the tavern so that we could eat, she would always know and chase us away. One of the other women working there would sneak us out some scraps." She closed her eyes, her face taking on a wistful appearance. "So much has changed in that time. Everything we know was destroyed, taken away in a battle that we couldn't even see."

The battle. That was what she needed to understand. What had happened to Ih-lash?

She had blamed the Hjan, but she had no proof of what had happened, only stories. Guya had heard some of them, but even he didn't know what had really happened.

"Tell me about the battle," Carth said.

"What's to say? Our father was shadow blessed, and he was called to serve when the attack came, forced to leave his shop. He never... he never saw it again." She swallowed, tears moistening his eyes. "Most of the shadow blessed were. None were trained to fight. Those who were part of the Reshian were informants. That was all."

"What of the Reshian?" They hadn't spoken of it, but there was anger in those who remained from Isahl about the Reshian. Carth needed to understand why.

"They were the soldiers of Ih-lash. They protected us, but eventually even they abandoned us."

"What of the shadow born? They can fight."

Lindy nodded. "Maybe they can fight, but should they?"

"What do you mean?"

"It only draws attention. When Andin discovered his ability, when he discovered the extent of what he could do, he wanted to fight. Father told him no, told him to keep me safe. There was only so much he could do. Then even Father disappeared."

"I haven't heard much about what happened during the battle."

Lindy turned away. "What is there to say? People died."

"I'd like to know what happened. My parents left the city, took me away from my homeland before I was old enough to even know why. Anything that can help me understand the reason…"

Lindy turned to her. "Your father was Reshian, wasn't he?"

Carth nodded. "I don't know if he was always Reshian or if he came to them after they discovered him. I thought that he wasn't, but when I found him alive, I realized there was more to him that I understood." That had been the part that had bothered her the most. How could he have hidden that from her? For that matter, how could he not have explained the rationale behind the games he always wanted to play with her?

"When the first attack came, the city turned on itself. There were those who were descendants of the Ih and those who are descendants of Lashasn, and both sides turned on each other."

"There was peace in Ih-lash," Carth said.

Lindy shook her head. "Maybe there once had been peace, but anything that existed has long been gone. Whatever else happened, the city destroyed itself before any further attacks came."

Carth imagined the descendants of Lashasn facing those of Ih, a battle much like that of the Reshian against the A'ras. She had thought that fight a newer battle, but what if it hadn't been? What if it was only an extension of the brutality that had existed in Ih-lash?

"Other attackers came after you escaped," Carth prompted when Lindy fell silent.

She nodded, her eyes going closed. "They came. They were... awful. There is no other way to describe it. So many had already suffered before those attacks reached our shores, so many were already lost. We didn't need another attack."

"What happened?" Carth asked.

"I... I don't know. We were shielded from most of it. Not all—there was no way to be protected from every-thing—but enough that we weren't aware of what happened. When additional attacks did come, they were violent and bloody, and the men who carried them out wore dark maroon robes. They were Lashasn."

Carth frowned. Maroon? That didn't sound like the Lashasn—or the A'ras. The descriptions reminded her more of what she had seen in the tavern, and on the ship where they had found the lost girls of the village.

She turned to Lindy but didn't get a chance to ask.

A pressure against her senses caught her attention.

It was a strange sensation, one that felt like she was being pushed, almost a physical touch, but nothing was near her. She took a deep breath that helped steady her connection to the different magics she possessed.

It took a moment, but she realized the source of the sensation. It was pressure against her connection to the shadows.

She frowned, staring into the darkness and into the

sea. As she did, she pulled on the shadows, wrapping them around her, cloaking her.

Lindy looked at her strangely. "Carth?"

Carth shook her head. "Do you see anything?"

To her credit, Lindy didn't question and simply stared into the darkness. She was shadow blessed and could use the shadows in ways that were similar to what Carth could do, but her talent was not quite as potent as either Carth's or Andin's.

She cloaked herself. Carth had rarely seen another use the shadows, and seeing Lindy fade in this way helped her know the other woman was using the shadows, and then she returned. "There is something there," Lindy said, "but I don't see what it is."

Carth turned away from the railing.

"Where you going?" Lindy asked.

"I've seen something like this before," Carth said. "The last time, many died. Guya and I both almost died. If this is the same, we need to be prepared."

She raced towards the helm of the ship and found Guya holding on to the wheel lightly, speaking softly to one of the shadow blessed. As Carth approached, the young girl scurried away.

Since picking up the additional crew, his mood had lightened somewhat. It was almost as if having only Carth and Dara on the ship had strained him. Now there were others, and he had taken to working with those of the shadow blessed who were willing to work with him. Some, like Andin, had no interest. But others, like a boy named Tom or this girl, had shown a willingness to work with Guya, almost eagerness.

"The blood magic. I feel something like it again."

Guya's eyes widened and he grabbed for his spyglass before scanning the horizon. With the darkness, Carth doubted he would see much. She considered using the spyglass, but doubted it would work with her shadow magic.

"Are you certain?"

"I feel it." The more she was aware of it, the more certain she became. This was the same sort of pressure she had felt when the ship had passed towards them the last time. Then, she had thought it had more to do with the fact that she had sunk so deeply into the shadows. Now she knew that wasn't exactly the case.

"You said they were resistant to your shadow magic," Guya said.

"The shadows didn't work, but the flame did. Without that…"

Guya surveyed his ship. Carth could almost imagine him counting the number of shadow blessed now aboard the ship. How many lives were in danger because of this blood magic?

"What do you want me to do?" he asked.

Carth shook her head. What was there to do? If they encountered the so-called blood priests while they were sailing, they would be forced to attack. That was no answer, not with everyone on board. If even a single one of them were placed in danger, it would be her fault.

Was there some way that they could turn away from this? Was there some way she could use the sensation she detected to avoid these blood priests?

She closed her eyes, wrapping herself thoroughly in

the shadows. As she did, she felt something like a dark cloud emanating away from her. She used the sensation, using the power she detected, and pushed out. It oozed away from her, something like a fog. In her mind, she could see the shadows. It wasn't real, but it gave her a sense of the sea, almost as if she could feel the waves as they washed beneath the shadows. Connected as she was this way, she felt the pressure. It came from the north and the west. The ship was moving fast, faster than the one they were on.

She opened her eyes. "Which direction are we headed?"

Guya nodded to the sky and pointed at a star. "That's the prince star. He guides us at night. Always to the south this time of year. We sailed towards the prince star and can continue heading south."

They needed speed. She could do it herself, but it might not be enough. They needed to get away from the blood priests. She feared what they might do to her were she captured, but she worried more about those she had rescued from Isahl. They were her responsibility now.

She hurried back to the railing and found Lindy. "Grab Andin. I need his help."

Lindy nodded and hurried off, disappearing below the deck of the ship.

Carth made her way to the stern. Wind moved around her, catching her dark hair so that it slapped her face. The spray coming off the sea did not affect her quite as much here. She shivered, cold from the gusting wind and the moisture in her cloak.

Reaching for as much of the shadow as she now

attempted was difficult, but she managed to grab onto them and pushed them behind her, using them to drive the ship forward. Now more than ever, she wanted to keep moving. Maybe reach the Reshian. They could help.

There was another option, but she doubted it was one the children of Isahl would agree to. They had barely agreed to come with her to find the Reshian. But if she could get them to Nyaesh, they would have others with them who could use the flame, and would be able to resist the blood priests.

Andin appeared. Outlined against the night sky, his muscular frame would've been attractive were it not for the dour expression he always carried and the anger she sensed within him.

"What did you want?"

Carth pointed behind her, motioning towards the north and where she sensed the pressure. "Use the shadows. Can you feel it?"

Lindy stood behind Andin, remaining near the mast. She did not come too close, but listened. Her face was a blank mask.

Andin approached carefully and stood at the railing without needing to hold on to it the way many of the other shadow blessed did. His eyes took on a faraway expression. Carth could feel him using the shadows, but couldn't detect what he did. There was nothing like the cloaking, nothing like what she'd seen from Lindy, but she was able to detect them used. Strange that she could even feel what he did.

"What is it?"

"I don't know who they are, but we call them the blood

priests." She continued to use the shadows and thrust behind her, driving the ship forward more quickly than it would move even with the powerful wind blowing them forward. "They use some sort of magic where they draw the blood of their victims across their skin. I fought several of them before reaching Isahl, but I don't know any more about them than that."

Andin glanced behind him to Lindy and they shared a look. Carth wondered what passed between them, and wondered what they might know about these blood priests.

"You know something."

Andin shook his head. "We don't know anything. We've seen those who can avoid our magic. We thought they were the descendants of Lashasn, but they use no flame. There is no heat. They come and they kill."

"I don't know what they are either, but they can avoid the shadows. They are able to overwhelm our magic. Between the two of us..."

Andin glanced once more to Lindy before returning his gaze back to Carth. "I will help."

The two of them worked, both of them wrapped in shadows and driving darkness behind them. As they did, Carth felt a growing speed from the ship. The presence of strange blood priests behind them gradually eased off of her shadow awareness.

Hours seemed to pass, though she doubted it had been that long. She lost track of time as they worked throughout the night. The sense of the ship began to ease, slowly leaving them, and Carth began to back off her connection to the shadows, exhaustion washing through her. Did Andin feel equally fatigued? If he did, he didn't show it.

When they got far enough away, Andin relaxed and released his connection to the shadows. He went with Lindy, and both disappeared below the deck of the ship, saying nothing more to her.

Carth stared into the distance behind the ship and towards the north. A nagging worry troubled her. Who were these blood priests, and why did they now pursue them?

CHAPTER 16

"They know something more than what they've told me, even if they don't know what that is."

Guya glanced at Carth, the sunlight reflecting in his eyes. He didn't look nearly as tired as she felt this morning, even though she knew he'd stood at the helm most of the night, steering them to safety. He didn't trust anyone else, and claimed not to need sleep. Carth wondered if the truth was that he could sleep standing up. She'd certainly seen him staring blankly a few times while traveling, making her suspect that was his secret.

After working throughout the night with Andin on driving the ship forward, she had sunk into her bunk, falling instantly asleep until being awoken by a particularly large wave that crashed into the ship, sending her rolling from her bunk and crashing to the floor. She rubbed the back of her neck, trying to work out the sore spot from falling, but it didn't work.

"You know that you're talking in circles? I thought I was the one who was tired."

"Guya—"

"What do you think they know?"

Carth looked over at the shadow blessed now arranged around the railing. They'd played games throughout the morning, some she'd recognized, and now she noted how Lindy worked with them, teaching several of the younger ones how to use the shadows. She was surprised to learn that she knew many of the same tricks. They practiced cloaking and releasing the cloaking, one after another. The boy whose name she now knew to be Ragan worked with Lindy, and together the two of them demonstrated their abilities with shadows. Andin had climbed into the crow's nest, hiding beneath the shadows of the highest sail, and she noted him watching both her and the students.

"They spoke of an attack on Ih-lash, one that sounds too much like what we saw with the blood priests."

Guya shook his head. "I've never seen anything like those attacks before. There are stories of power, but none where people are slaughtered and their blood utilized to make their killers stronger. It would be a dangerous sort of magic, especially considering who else might want it."

What would have happened if the Hjan had been able to use blood magic or the A'ras flame during the attack? They might have had the strength to withstand attacks. The blood priests were able to withstand her shadow magic, and she had seen the Hjan withstand her shadows using something like a flash of light to burn them from her, but during the accords, they hadn't been able to do so. She didn't know if she had gotten stronger or they had lost the ability.

Then there was the fact that the Hjan had appeared in Lonsyn.

Why else would they have been there unless there was something for them to learn? Everything she had been taught about the Hjan told her that they sought power. What better source of power than those who could use the blood of their victims to gain increasing strength? She could imagine the Hjan using such power and gaining great strength, possibly enough to overwhelm both the remaining Reshian and the A'ras.

"I don't think we can make it to the Reshian before they reach us," she said, focusing her shadow connection behind the ship. She maintained a faint connection to the shadows even while sleeping. Doing so had allowed her to remain aware of the location of the ship that trailed them. It slowly closed on them, but they still had to reach the river and navigate down those waters before reaching Nyaesh. If the blood priests reached them prior to that…

"What choice do we have but to continue to sail?" Guya asked.

"We can fight, or we can run. Those are our options."

Guya turned his attention to the shadow-blessed students working in the bow. "We can't risk them," he said softly. "They've suffered enough already. We need to be able to do something to protect them. Isn't that why you brought them from Isahl?"

What she really needed was to find a connection to the Reshian. If she could find them, she would be able to provide protection. She might even be able to provide additional training. Andin seemed disinterested in working with the students. He was powerful, and had helped them escape the night before, but he was reserved, and that reservation was dangerous.

Of course, Carth needed to spend more time working with the students as well—almost as much for herself as for them. There was much she might be able to learn from those who trained with shadow blessed. They knew of the games her parents had taught her, games that were the key to understanding the secrets of the shadow blessed.

"How far are we from Nyaesh?"

Guya arched a brow. "Is that your plan now?"

"Only if nothing else works."

"A dangerous gambit. You know what happened to them. They already think Lashasn attacked."

"What choice do we have?"

Guya breathed out heavily. "I don't know."

Guya reached into his pocket and pulled out a folded and faded map. Carth had seen it from a distance a few times during her travels, but Guya usually watched over it protectively. On the map were the positions of different islands, with the large mass of land in the center representing the northern continent. Nyaesh, accessed only by the Malenth River, sat near the center. To the far north, near a bay labeled in old Ih, she saw Isahl represented. A large island sat at the northern section of the bay, representing the original Lashasn.

Guya's smoothed the map on a flat section of the rail near the helm. He pointed at it with a thick finger, which he traced along the coast, running from Isahl down towards the mouth of the river.

"We're here," he said, pointing towards a section of the map that was still farther north than she'd thought they had sailed. His finger traced along the map into the river. "This section is a little more treacherous. We have to move around rocks and reefs. I've sailed them a few times... but these seas can be dangerous. They call them the Lost Seas."

"Lost?"

"Ships. Hundreds of ships crash around here."

Carth studied the map. Guya was a skilled captain and seemed to know his limitations, but she didn't want to risk sinking by rushing.

"Once we reach the mouth of the river, it would probably only be a few days depending on the winds," he went on. "The return trip would be faster, but of course then we have the current with us."

Carth stared at the map. It'd been years since she'd seen a map quite this detailed. Her father had once possessed one, and he had sat looking down at the map at night. She remembered her mother working in the kitchen, quietly cooking or mixing combination of herbs and leaves and oils, making her various concoctions that she used for healing or to sell. She had never understood why her father stared at the map the way he did, but she'd thought he was planning their next move in a game she hadn't understood. Even while in Nyaesh, he had still looked at the map each night.

Carth closed her eyes, reaching through the shadows and feeling the connection to them. It was more difficult in the sunlight, but with this connection, she could reach far from herself. She delved beneath the sea, pulling shadows from the depths that she could use to stretch all the way towards the blood priests' ship. It moved quickly against the waves, pounding through them, almost as if driven by the power of the sun.

They didn't use the A'ras flame, and they were not Lashasn. Still… they were powerful. They were dangerous. And she agreed with Guya that she needed to keep the children of Ih-lash alive. They might be the last children of Ih.

"Would there be any way to lose them in the Lost Sea?"

Guya stared at the map, his eyes intent. He circled a section of the sea with his finger. "We won't find the Reshian that way."

"Not at first," she said.

Guya nodded. "This part… this section of the sea is more dangerous than any other. Some of the older sailors call this the Elders Jaw."

"Why is that?"

"This is the part of the sea where most of the ships have been lost. Countless lives as well. Countless more have been damaged, taking on water only to come limping into shore and require extensive repairs. My own ship took a gash in the bow the last time we came through here—part of the reason I had refused to sail here in the past."

A plan started forming in Carth's mind. Could they lose blood priests in the Elders Jaw part of the sea? If they could, what did that buy them?

Not answers. And answers were something she wanted.

A part of her wished she hadn't been so aggressive

with them when they had attacked the ship the last time. Had she only been willing to keep the captive, she might've been able to get answers. Of course, then she hadn't known that there might be a connection to Ih-lash.

The only other option was for her to somehow reach the other ship and see what she could do.

Did it have to be only her?

What if she had someone else to help?

She glanced down at the shadow blessed working on the bow. They all seemed so… innocent. They worked on cloaking and sinking into the shadows but didn't have the experience of facing someone willing to murder them. They had suffered enough in Isahl, and she didn't want to be responsible for bringing them back into that horror.

No. She couldn't use them to help.

Her gaze turned to the crow's nest, and she thought about Andin. As another of the shadow born, he would be an option as well, but she doubted he would be interested in working with her. Besides that, if they were to get ahold of him and his ability, Ih-lash would lose another shadow born. More than that, she didn't know if the blood magic gained anything from the powers of those they took it from. What if they could use the blood of the shadow born's to gain increased strength?

That raised a different question. What of those who had died in the tavern in Lonsyn?

Was that the reason behind what they'd found there?

Too many questions. She had no answers, something that frustrated her. How could she make the right move if she had no idea what pieces were moving? Worse, the

pieces that moved around her seemed to have more information than she did.

If not the shadow blessed, the only other option
involved Dara. Carth wasn't entirely sure she wanted to
bring the woman with her. The last time she had been
involved, she'd jumped to violence and anger. Carth
understood now that it was violence that had been
deserved, but at the time, Dara hadn't known that. She'd
acted based on assumptions rather than understanding.

If only Dara were better able to plan and strategize.
She had thought by playing Tsatsun with her, she might
be able to teach her, but so far Dara hadn't progressed. It
was a game that required patience and foresight, but so
far Dara had not demonstrated either of those traits.

She shook her head. She would give Dara another
chance. She had to; Dara possessed the power of the S'al,
and that seemed to be something the blood priests were
unable to withstand.

Carth patted Guya on the shoulder and let out a long
sigh, pointing to the map. "Make your way towards the
Elders Jaw. If what I plan doesn't work, you'll need to lose
them there."

"And what do you plan?"

"I intend to play a game with Dara."

"And if that doesn't work?"

She shook her head. "If that doesn't work, then it will
have to be up to me."

Guya frowned at her. "This doesn't always have to
come on your shoulders, Carth. You're powerful, I've seen
that, but others can work with you."

She smiled. "Others do work with me. That's why I

have you." She nodded towards the shadow-blessed students working on the bow. "That's why we brought them on board. I don't intend to do this myself, not once we gain enough assets."

"Assets? That's what they are to you?"

She sighed again. "Assets. Pieces in a game. Either way, it's a game I intend to win."

CHAPTER 17

CARTH SAT ACROSS FROM DARA, ONCE MORE PLAYING A game of Tsatsun. She had made a point of explaining to her the intent of the game, hoping that if she shared with Dara what she intended to accomplish, Dara would understand the importance of maintaining her focus and thinking accordingly. So far, the game had not gone well for her.

"You move impatiently," Carth said.

She held on to the connection to the shadows, delving beneath the sea with them as she stretched her awareness to the north, tracking after the distant blood priest ship. They were still there, distant but growing steadily closer, almost as if they were fully aware of how to find the *Goth Spald*. Carth had to believe that they *might* know.

"Impatient? This is how I was taught to play," Dara said.

"Then you were taught wrong. The intent is to move the stone, not destroy the other side."

"If you remove the other pieces, you can move the stone more easily," Dara said.

Carth motioned to the pile of pieces she had claimed from Dara. "It does, but if you don't plan well enough, you'll never get the opportunity to capture the pieces. You have to be able to move well enough before you can start attacking. Then you can make your attempt on the stone."

She made a few movements, each of them getting closer and closer to the stone. Each time she did, Dara seemed oblivious to what she attempted. Rather than ending it—which would probably have been a mercy—she played it out, taking more time than was necessary. By the end of the game, Dara had almost no pieces remaining and stared at the board as if trying to understand what she might have missed. There was a time when Carth had had the same reaction, but that had been during the first few games she'd ever played. Since then, she'd gotten more skilled.

She now understood what Ras had said about not having someone to play with. Winning too easily was worse than losing. At least with losing, she was forced to think through what she'd done wrong and try to come up with a different strategy the next time.

Carth moved the stone, ending the game.

"Again," she said, setting up the board.

This time had gone better than the last. Dara managed to demonstrate *some* anticipation. She still played eagerly, and without regard for caution, but she had progressed for the first time ever during their sessions. Carth had made a point of explaining why she made each move, hoping that through her explanations, Dara would be able to anticipate or at least think through what she intended. So far, she hadn't.

Even sharing her strategy, Carth still won easily. Had she played someone who had a modicum of skill, she would have struggled, though the idea of announcing her moves amused her. Would she be able to announce them and still win? It might add to the level of difficulty, especially if she described what she would do the next two or three steps ahead.

Dara slouched in her chair. "I'm terrible."

Carth nodded. "You're not good yet. That's the point of playing."

"I don't think I'll ever be able to compete at your level."

Carth didn't think that likely either, but telling Dara that would only deflate her even more. Instead, she said, "You need more practice, and you need to recognize where you *can* move, and where you need to be more cautious. But you did play better this time."

"I focused on the stone," Dara said.

"I noticed."

"You did?"

"It was the first time I didn't think you were simply trying to pile up pieces."

Carth sat back and looked at the game board. She wished Dara could play with more efficiency and more forethought, but that wasn't her skill.

Was there a way to play *to* Dara's skill?

She set the pieces back on the board and began

arranging them. As she did, Dara stared at it, focused on the stone. Her face contorted as if she were trying to determine how to move the piece with her mind, rather than coaxing it with the other pieces. They didn't even need to be strong pieces. Any move would have been enough to convince her.

"That's your problem," Carth said. "You're so focused on the stone that you forget to play the other pieces."

Dara shook her head. "It's not that I forget to play the pieces, it's that you told me I needed to focus on the stone to win. Before, I focused on removing the other person's pieces. That was how I was taught to play."

Carth considered her words, thinking about how she could encourage her to play a different strategy. She'd explained looking at the game from another's perspective, but that hadn't helped Dara.

What would she be able to tell her that would help her reach her potential with the game? Dara would never be a master at Tsatsun, but it *was* possible for her to get better. Carth believed it was possible for *anyone* to get better, especially with practice and an understanding of strategy.

"Why don't you focus on the stone and play with only the Rangers this time?" Carth suggested.

"Why only the Rangers?"

Carth started removing pieces from the game board. She removed pieces of hers as well as pieces of Dara's. When all were gone other than the Rangers, she motioned to the board. "Humor me. Let's work on these, focus on using only these pieces, and see how well you play the game."

Dara made her first move, moving one of the Rangers

from the back of the board and taking it at an angle. It was a bold move, one that she was not surprised to see coming from Dara.

Carth played a tentative game intentionally, wanting to feel out how she would play. She wasn't sure if Dara would play with more patience than she had before, and was pleased to discover that Dara could focus on the task more easily when she was only moving the single type of piece.

Maybe the problem for Dara wasn't so much the complexity of the game but the distractions that could be found within it.

It was easy to get caught up in the potential found within the game. Early on, when playing and training with Ras, Carth had discovered ways of holding all the different patterns in her head, but Dara was not Carth, and it was necessary for Carth not to treat her the same way.

Dara surprised Carth with a move and reached towards the stone, making a move as if to nudge it forward and onto Carth's side of the board. She let out an excited little yelp.

Carth smiled, and she let Dara play her pieces a little longer before countering, leaving them in a draw, with their pieces surrounding the stone in the middle of the board. Carth could have defeated her completely, but that would only have taken away a sense of victory. Sometimes believing in victory was enough to help with under-standing.

Carth sat back and crossed her arms over her chest, a half-smile crossing her face. "That was much better. You were able to focus on the task at hand instead of getting distracted by all of the other pieces."

"What was the point of removing the other pieces?"

"The point was focusing your play."

"I wasn't focused before?"

"Did you win?"

Dara sighed, eyes still locked on the stone. Carth could tell she was pleased with herself. Hadn't Carth felt the same way the first time she'd thought she'd beaten Ras?

"The Rangers... was it all about removing distraction?"

She understood. That was good. "I've told you how Tsatsun will often reveal things about the player. I've learned you're impatient, and that you prefer to attack. I'm the same way. But I've learned that you lose focus. There are times when I might need you to be able to accomplish a goal. Other pieces will move around you, and you will need to be able to counter them, and to focus on what you're asked to do."

Dara looked up from the board, her brow furrowed as she made the connection. "And what do you intend to ask me to do?"

Carth smiled. Dara recognized there was more to this exercise. Maybe she *could* learn.

"The blood priests continue to pursue us. I can feel them pressing on my shadow senses. Andin and I were able to press them back last night and gain time, but we weren't able to stop them. We could continue to push them back and race towards Nyaesh, but I don't want to bring the children of Isahl to Nyaesh if I don't have to."

"But you would?"

"If I have to."

"Why?"

Carth sighed. "There's more to the destruction of Ih-lash than I realized. I thought it was all due to the Hjan but I don't think that's all there was. They blame Lashasn for a second attack. What if the blood priests had something to do with it?"

"Those weren't blood priests you found in the tavern in Lonsyn."

"I'm not sure what they were, but they weren't your typical tavern people either." She thought of the man that the green-eyed Hjan had been most focused on. She didn't know why he had wanted him, but there had to be something about the bodies that had drawn the Hjan. They had risked coming to Lonsyn, risked facing Carth.

The accords would hold, but what was it they were after? What power did they think to gain?

"What now?" Dara asked.

Carth stood. She had seen what she needed to see from Dara. She agreed with Guya that she couldn't face attacks like this on her own. She had barely survived when it came to the accords, and she hadn't faced anything quite like these blood priests. She didn't know enough about them to effectively counter them, which was part of the reason she intended to reach their ship and find out what she could, learn how they played. She had to, if she intended to bring the shadow-blessed youth to safety.

"Now it's time for you and I to attack."

CHAPTER 18

CARTH AND DARA SAT IN THE DINGHY, PERCHED ATOP THE hard wooden seats, waves roiling around them and slowly pushing them away from Guya and his ship. Carth convinced Andin and Lindy to use their connection to the shadows and hold on to them while they were gone. Carth could trace that back to the *Goth Spald*. Of course, that depended on them surviving.

"How far are we?" Dara asked. She was dressed in loose-fitting pants and a well-cut shirt, one that had drawn the attention of Andin as they had jumped onto the dinghy. Dara carried two knives at her waist as well, matching Carth in that way. They were well-forged knives, made of a strange dark silvery metal and branded with a particular mark at the end of the blade. Guya claimed he had found them on the southern continent and stated that there had once been more knives like this, but now they were rare.

Carth closed her eyes. She could feel the shadows

pressing against the ship far in the distance. When she stretched with them the opposite way, towards the south, she was able to feel the growing distance of the *Goth Spald*.

Would they reach it again? Would it matter if they didn't learn about this blood magic? They needed to find out more about these blood priests, something that would help her keep the others safe.

Through the shadows, Carth was able to contact the presence of the oncoming ship.

It sliced through the water but, more importantly, it also sliced through her connection to the shadows.

"Can you reach your connection to the S'al?"

"I can," Dara said.

Carth traced her finger across the ring she wore on her middle finger, the one that she had taken from her mother. Barbs pressed into the flesh of her finger, but she had discovered this connected her more deeply to her shadow power. Through this, she was able to draw upon the flame without the same resistance she'd met when training in Nyaesh. With this, she wondered if she could actually have risen higher with the A'ras. Maybe then she might have felt as if she belonged.

Carth sat back on the seat of the dinghy. Her eyes lost focus as she paid attention to the sense of the shadows. It was late, and she had chosen this time intentionally, wanting the shadows to protect her as they approached, but now she wondered if daylight might've been better. She might not have had the same protection with the shadows, but she would've had some advantage with the S'al. That was the key to victory, and Dara and she both had that advantage over the blood priests. Did she lose something by coming at night?

Both of them worked the oars, using Carth's connection to the shadows to propel them towards the blood priest's ship. Neither spoke, but both knew their tasks. Dara understood that when they reached the ship, her task was to sink it, using her connection to the S'al to ignite it.

Carth didn't worry about her own safety. She could protect herself from the flame and that the night and the shadows would keep her safe—so long as the blood priests couldn't dissipate it. Perhaps that was reason enough for them to come in the night, so that she could use the shadows, so that she could have that advantage over them.

Nearly an hour passed before she could see the ship in the distance.

Carth shifted her focus with the shadows, now drawing them around the dinghy, using them to cloak the small vessel. They continued to row, and Carth used the shadows to propel them forward, closer and closer to the other ship.

Dara leaned close to her and whispered, "If they know the *Goth Spald* is to the south, does it make sense for us to come from this direction?"

Carth smiled. Dara was actually using strategy. Perhaps she *could* learn. "I intend for them to know that we're coming."

"Won't that only draw their attack?"

Carth nodded. "I need to know what they are capable

of. Right now, I have no idea, other than that they have brute strength and they're hard to kill."

Dara rubbed her arms and shivered. "This really is like a game of Tsatsun to you, isn't it?"

"Everything is a game," Carth said.

The dinghy slowly parted the water, gradually approaching the larger ship. Carth could feel increasing agitation against the shadows, as if the blood priests became more aware of her presence. Would they know that Dara came as well?

She had to test them. There was one way to do that well enough for her to think they would respond.

She pulled upon the shadows, drawing them around her in a thick fog of a cloak. With the shadows, she was able to feel the way the blood priests worked against her magic, the same way that it worked when they sailed through it. It was a brutal sort of power, one she felt practically pulsing against her.

This was nothing like fighting the Hjan.

At least with the Hjan, she knew what she was facing, knew that they could flicker and disappear. With these blood priests, she was ignorant. It was time that changed.

"Stay down," she said to Dara. She didn't want the other woman discovered by the blood priests yet. She would rather have them think that she was alone. That gave them an advantage of surprise, an extra piece that she could move against them.

Dara dropped into the bow of the boat, and Carth pulled upon the shadows, using them to conceal Dara. They drifted forward, propelled by her magic.

The ship slipped through the waves, cutting through

them with more strength than Carth would have expected. Was there something about the ship itself?

It was too dark to know, but she could imagine them painting it with blood, much like the sails had seemed painted. It crashed through the sea, as if powered by something other than the wind.

As they neared, she parted the shadows to look up at the tall deck of the ship. High above her, she noted at least three men standing on the bow of a ship, men who looked nothing like the Reshian. There was something about them that tugged on familiarity, though she wasn't certain why.

This close, she could make out details she couldn't from farther away. Each of them wore long dark robes that reminded her more of the men in the tavern than those from the ship attack. These men had a more refined appearance, with long, elegant features, and they had eyes that were a flat gray, almost a steel. Their skin was pale, almost sallow and saggy in appearance that looked as if they had never seen the sun. Hands that gripped the railing were stained maroon.

There was no question. These were the blood priests.

They were different than those she'd seen on the ship before. She suspected their ability was the same, as was the capacity to ignore the shadows, almost as if her ability was made useless. Would they use blood in the same way?

With the thought, the nearest man, a tall one with dark wrinkles along the corners of his eyes who was concealed in shadows cast by the hood of his cloak, waved his hand and the shadows around her vanished.

Carth had never experienced anything quite like that.

Was that what Isahl had faced?

When she'd faced Ras, he had used the power of the S'al to suppress her ability with the shadows. He had managed to tear them from her with light and pain, but had also managed to suppress her ability with the S'al by drawing away heat and warmth.

This was nothing like that. This was simply a dispersement of the shadows.

Dara was exposed without the shadows to conceal her and keep her safe. Without her ability, there was nothing Carth could do. That advantage was removed.

Carth began thinking in terms of gamesmanship. They had made a strong move, and now it was her turn to either make an equally strong maneuver or counter in an unexpected way.

Carth glanced to the bottom of the boat. Dara could be useful here, but she would need her to focus and to maintain her attack in a way that Carth was not entirely certain that the other woman would able to do.

"We have a change in plan," Carth said. "I need you to focus your attack on that lead man there." She pointed to the man nearest her. "Do you see him? Did you see the way he waved away the shadows?"

"I never see the shadows in the first place. All I can see is the darkness swirling around us like a fog."

"They've dispersed the shadows. I suspect I'll have minimal shadow ability around them."

Dara cast a furtive gaze in her direction. "Are you certain we should do this? What if they—"

"I am not dependent upon only one ability."

As she readied to attack, she hesitated.

A memory of a lesson taught to her, by Jhon and by Ras, came to the forefront of her mind. She couldn't be too dependent upon her abilities. That was the reason she had been trapped by Ras in the past. She'd used planning and a little bit of luck to defeat the Hjan when they'd settled the accords, but with these men, she needed answers before she risked herself to destroy them.

She shifted her shadow ability towards the stern of the dinghy and used it to propel them around the back of the larger ship.

She noted with satisfaction how the lead man followed her. He didn't seem to know what to make of the fact that she wasn't attacking as she suspected he anticipated.

"How am I going to attack him if we're back here?"

Carth nodded towards the ship. "Stay in this dinghy. I'm going on board. Be ready to attack, but don't attempt to climb on board. I suspect they'll be stronger than you'll be able to resist."

Dara looked at Carth with disbelieving eyes. "You're going to leave me here? What happens if one of them reaches me?"

"For this to work, I think we need to work together. I can't do this alone, but I don't want to risk you getting harmed."

"This is what you been teaching me for. I'm ready to help you—"

"No. Keep your focus as we discussed. Think of it like the game."

"This isn't a game. This is you risking yourself."

"Isn't it? Everything you need to know about strategy and battling, you can learn from the game of Tsatsun.

Even this. Attack. Counter. Move again. They are the same."

Carth began drawing on her S'al magic, using the power she could bind through the ring, and let this fill her. Dara did the same, practically glowing. Did Carth glow like Dara did?

Carth unsheathed her knives. She might not be able to use the knives with shadows, but she could certainly use the knife Invar had given her to draw strength and focus her S'al magic.

With the powerful leap, she burst from the dinghy and reached the back railing of the other ship. Carth threw herself over the railing and into a battle. Five blood priests immediately surrounded her. Each of them had streaks of dark maroon dried on their cheeks. Their fingers were stained as well. They stunk, a bitter and foul odor that emanated from them. Three of the men had no shirts and their chests were covered with dried maroon blood. *These* were more like the men from the ship.

"Reshian." This came from a small woman with skin as pale as that of the man on the bow of the ship. Her face was like wax and seemed to drip. Pockmarks dotted her cheeks, as if she had been sick as a child and scarred. Her eyes had a steely gray to them similar to the other man's, but she didn't carry the same age, and stood before Carth empty-handed. "We have captured most of your ships. Were you on one that got away?"

Carth hesitated. Was that why she hadn't seen any of the Reshian ships?

She pushed the thought away, taking a quick survey, and realized they all faced her without weapons.

She darted forward, slashing with her A'ras knife.

As the lead attacker reached for her arm, Carth jumped back, flipping as she did, and brought her foot around to connect with the man behind her, catching him on the temple. He fell forward, striking the railing. Carth flipped her heel around, and he went over the edge and into the water with a splash.

She offered a quick prayer, hoping Dara wouldn't make the mistake of attempting to attack.

Four attackers remained.

They closed in on her, and as they did, she became aware of their foul odor and felt pressure against her. She had been holding on to a connection to the shadows. Whatever they did with the shadows weakened her.

She released them and focused solely on her Lashasn connection to the S'al.

"A powerful Reshian," the little woman said. "You will make a fine addition. We have claimed enough of the Reshian, but few have the power you display. There was one, but he managed to escape us."

The blood priests closed in on her.

Now was the time for her to change her approach.

She had told Dara the truth about Tsatsun. If nothing else, it informed everything she did. She needed to understand what they were capable of. There was only one way to do it.

They took a step closer.

She waited.

Another step.

Behind them, the older blood priest neared. She could practically feel power coming off him, almost as if in waves. He watched her, his gaze unreadable. Carth knew she needed to draw them in, but that didn't change the flutter of fear and the worry that she'd made a mistake.

Dropping to the deck, she swung her legs around in a quick arc.

Carth had been trained by the A'ras, and she used this training to deadly effect. As the first man fell, she slashed with her knife, her blade flashing with S'al magic.

She continued in a rapid sweep, knocking the blood priests down and stabbing with the S'al. Each time she did, they screamed.

Leaping to her feet, she saw that only a few of the blood priests remained. She noted the woman and the older man, but a third, one she didn't recognize from earlier, stood near the helm of the ship. He watched, almost as if disinterested.

With certainty, she knew that was the man to fear.

Carth jumped at the woman. The blood priest caught her wrist and threw her to the ground. Carth exploded upward, fueled by the S'al magic, and spun. When she landed, she kicked, catching the woman in the back so that she staggered forward.

Turning to the older man, she watched with a horrified fascination as he pulled a jar of blood from beneath his cloak. He opened the top and poured it over himself.

Thick maroon blood cascaded down his cheeks and into the folds of his neck, catching in the wrinkles of his face.

He changed before her.

She had no other way to describe what happened. Muscles built beneath his flesh, pushing them outward.

She had thought his features sallow and sagging and wrinkled, but all that disappeared under the blood magic.

The other man, the man she assumed captain of the ship, did something similar, though his jar was larger and his transformation more terrifying.

The woman pulled herself to her feet and used a similar jar of blood, but—more horrifying than the other two—poured it into her mouth, letting it run over her cheeks and down her chin.

All three of them changed into enormous creatures like something out of a nightmare. One she could have faced by herself; three were more than she could handle.

"You will be powerful, Reshian," the older man said. His voice was deep and had a rasp that grated on her ears. "We will empty your blood into our basins and sing songs of your death as we use your blood to destroy the rest of your kind."

It was all Carth needed to know.

She pulled upon the power she possessed from the S'al magic, drawing through the ring. Taking the knife, pulling as much power as she could, she slammed it into the deck of the ship.

This was Invar's knife, one he had given her, crafted for her to match the one her father had possessed. It was a perfectly weighted blade, and one she valued, one that had been a marker of all her time in Nyaesh. It was a focus. Once upon a time, Invar had thought she needed the focus. Now Carth no longer did. She had her mother's ring. She understood Lashasn magic. She understood the S'al. Now what she needed was to forge her own knife if she was to embrace that side of her.

But it was a focus.

She pressed all the power of the S'al through the knife, and through the connection she possessed.

It began glowing, taking on a brilliant white light. It seared the wood of the deck around it. The power of the knife pressed back the three transformed blood priests.

More than that, it began burning a hole through the ship.

Carth jumped, letting the force of her magic carry her out over the water and hopefully into the dinghy waiting below, where she crashed into the sea.

As she sank below the surface, she pressed all her S'al magic into the focus of Invar's knife she'd left plunged into the deck. It burned against her senses and exploded in a ball of fire and light.

Carth burst out of the water. Dara sat on the dinghy only a boat length from her. She swam toward her, but as she tried climbing into the boat, something grabbed her.

Carth spun, remembering the man she had kicked off the ship. She slashed with her shadow knife, knowing it would have little effect against him with his blood magic. All she could hope was that the blood magic would be countered by the water, washing it from him.

A wave smashed into him and dragged him away from their small dinghy.

Carth clung to the edge of the dinghy, kicking to drive it forward, pulling shadows with her and streaking them through the water. The farther they got from the now-burning blood priest ship, the more she was able to relax.

Carth settled in the bottom of the dinghy, breathing heavily.

Dara watched her. "What… what happened there?"

Carth smiled to herself. "We made our move. Now it's time to see what they do to counter."

"What will we do?"

In this case, the obvious answer was the right one. The blood priests had admitted they had killed off the Reshian, which made finding them more difficult than she had anticipated. That left her with the other plan, the one she knew those of Isahl wouldn't approve of—but what choice did they have if they wanted to be safe?

"We will go to Nyaesh."

CHAPTER 19

THE INSIDE OF THE *GOTH SPALD* WAS DIM ENOUGH TO LET her see the soft glow coming off Dara. She possessed such power with her connection to the S'al that it made it so she practically exuded power, enough that she could barely contain it. Carth doubted that she possessed the same glow as Dara did.

She pushed open the door to their room. It was a small space, but then, everything on the *Spald* was small. The ship was fast, which was why Guya liked it, but that meant it was narrow of hull. Inside the room, Lindy sat next to Andin and two of the others from Isahl. She looked up when Carth entered, as if she'd been waiting for her to appear.

"I'd like to talk to Lindy," Carth said to Andin. She would convince her first. Then she would explain to Andin what they needed to do.

"Not by herself. I'm going to stay."

"Do you think I'm going to do something to hurt her?"

Carth asked. "Haven't I shown you that I'm working with you?"

Lindy touched his arm. "This is Carth, Andin. She's one of us."

"She's one of them, too."

"Which is why I want the accords to hold," Carth said.

Andin stared at her. "If you harm her—"

Lindy laughed, surprising Carth. "Do you think you could do anything to her? You've seen her fight. There's nothing either of us could do when it comes to her. Go to the surface and wait for me. I'll be fine."

He sighed but stood, pulling the others with him.

When they were gone, Carth closed the door and sat across from Lindy. She was dark-haired and dark-eyed, and because of that, quite lovely.

"How did you stay safe when Isahl was attacked the last time?" Was there anything there that would help them stop the blood priests?

"It was like they knew to target those with shadow skill. Andin protected us. The rest of us… we can use the shadows, but we're not like you and Andin."

"I don't think that's quite true. I saw how you could use the shadows. There's one with you who disappeared in them."

"Disappearing is only a trick, and one too many know how to look through. These attackers must have known."

"Which is why Andin thinks the attack was A'ras."

"Lashasn, but yes."

"Lashasn has been destroyed the same as Ih. There is no more Lashasn. The people of that land have scattered."

"You have one with you on this ship. You must

descend from one as well, or else you wouldn't have the abilities you do."

"Descended, but then my parents were of Ih-lash," Carth reminded her. "I'm trying to work through what happened and how to prevent another attack, but I will need your help. And your cooperation."

"Why?"

"I'm struggling with the process," Carth admitted.

"My mother used to teach me a game when I needed to focus my mind," Lindy said.

Carth smiled. "My father taught me plenty of games." But then, he had been shadow born as well. She still didn't know if he had known that she was, but maybe it didn't matter anyway.

"You are of Ih. You should have known the games."

"I didn't know they were something everyone learned," Carth said. "For me, they were my father's way of keeping me safe when we visited new cities. We moved around so much that we needed to have a way of keeping us safe." It was something she thought fondly of, even if her father had never shared with her why he had taught her the games. She had only known them as a way to keep safe. She would hide when needed, or learn how to find him. Never anything more than that, and certainly she had never imagined that he was teaching her to use some magical ability. Had she known that, would she have put more effort into it?

"What did you learn?" Lindy asked.

"The earliest was simply a game where he had me follow him. The goal was to remain hidden so that he didn't know that I did. I was never as good with him as I was with my mother."

"I imagine he was shadow blessed at least," Lindy said.

Carth nodded. Now wasn't the time to reveal that her father was part of the Reshian, and it certainly wasn't the time to reveal that he was shadow born, not only shadow blessed.

"Did he name it?" Lindy asked.

Carth shook her head. "None of the games had a name."

"We call what you describe the Skulking. It is the first of many, but the basis for so much. Many never progress beyond the Skulking. Mastering it is difficult, even for the blessed."

"We played it every day."

"You are lucky."

"Why is that?"

"To practice with another shadow blessed, even once a week, is considered lucky. There are too many to work with, too many to determine whether they are only able to detect the shadows, or whether they are something more. Few get even that much time, and you were able to practice daily."

Carth had never considered that side of it before. Of course, they would have worked to train others with the shadows. Had her father been selfish in taking her from Ih-lash? If he could train others, what kind of loss had his disappearance been for the people of her homeland? More than that, he was shadow born. Losing that ability would be even more of a loss for Ih-lash.

"Did you progress beyond skulking?" Lindy asked.

"There were several others. He taught me to find him when hidden, or he would shadow me and I would have to discover him."

Lindy nodded. "The Fade and the Thief."

Carth smiled. Learning that her games had names made them playful in some ways, nothing like the way her parents had used them. There had been some playfulness to the games, but nothing like what these names made them seem. Would she have embraced them differently had they been named? To her, they had been the way she had interacted with her parents, and with her father in particular. Her mother had never played any games like this, only fostering what her father had done, helping him to teach her.

"How far did you progress?" Carth asked.

"I almost mastered skulking before…"

Before the attack. Before the Hjan came and destroyed Ih-lash. Before.

"You mentioned your mother taught you a game to focus your mind. What was that game?"

Lindy brushed back loose strands of dark hair and leaned forward with a sigh. "She had a game she called Tsatsun. Few know of it, at least around where I was raised. Mother said it was a game she learned from her grandmother."

Carth smiled and raised a hand. "Wait here."

She hurried from the room and returned with her Tsatsun board. When she started setting it up, Lindy watched her with wide eyes. "How is it that you know how to play this? Did your father teach you this as well?"

Carth shook her head. "As far as I can tell, this is a

game from Lashasn. I learned it from a man who considered himself a master."

Carth quickly got the board set up and made the first move. Would Lindy be any more skilled than Dara?

"Lashasn? No, that can't be right. As I said, my grandmother taught me."

"Then your grandmother was descended from Lashasn. You were in Ih-lash. It shouldn't be surprising that there are others with that history there."

"My grandmother would not have been from Lashasn," she said softly.

"Why? The people of Ih and those of Lashasn came together long ago."

"I know the story of Carthenne."

Carth smiled. "Good. Then you understand why I want to ensure that peace remains."

"You think you can recreate what Carthenne of old did?"

"I think I can ensure that there is some lasting peace. I don't know what else I can achieve, but peace. That seems like something I *can* do."

She made a move on the board and waited.

Lindy watched her, her mouth folding into a tight frown. Would she be able to get over the same prejudice she carried from her time in Isahl, or would she continue to struggle against it?

Lindy nodded, almost to herself, and slid a piece across the board.

Carth knew the move and allowed her to play it out. She could think of nearly a dozen different ways that such a move could help, and a dozen where it would be nothing more than a demonstration of ignorance. Which one would it be for Lindy?

As they played, Carth discovered that Lindy had progressed far more than Dara. She didn't consider it a criticism of Dara, only that Lindy had more advanced moves, and she seemed to recognize what Carth did.

It still didn't stop Carth from defeating her, but it did give Carth a chance to determine what Lindy might know, and how she might play. The woman had potential, if only she would be willing to use it.

"Does your brother play?" Carth said as she began putting the pieces back into the container she used to store them.

"Andin?" Lindy shook her head. "Andin has never had the right patience for this. He'll play, but he gets frustrated when he can't win."

"Tsatsun can do that to people. It's easy to get upset when you don't have success."

"Where did you learn to play like that?" Lindy asked.

"Odian. There's a man there who taught me."

"I think you could even have beaten my grandmother," she said.

Carth wondered if that was a compliment and decided to take it as one.

"What now?" Lindy asked.

"Now we need to stop additional attacks."

"I thought you didn't know how to find them."

Carth tapped the Tsatsun board, her fingers drumming along the slick surface, tracing from one square to the next. Doing this soothed her and helped her focus. What she needed was a way to place all the pieces that were coming together in a specific order in her mind so that she could play the game out in a way that would help her understand what she might be missing. If only this was a game.

"I don't. Not entirely. But there's something we can do to stop the blood priests. I've seen the key to stopping them."

"What is it?"

"Fire."

Lindy stared at the board before looking up to Carth. "You would have us risk them."

"There is no risk." Carth didn't think there would be, but what if the A'ras didn't agree to offer protection?

"Lashasn attacked—"

Carth breathed out. "It wasn't Lashasn. Lindy… I need your help with this. We need to stop these blood priests, and the Reshian can't help."

"And Lashasn can?"

"The A'ras use fire. It works against the priests."

Lindy stared at the Tsatsun board, as if searching for answers. After a while, she nodded. "I will convince them." She looked up, meeting Carth's eyes. "That is what you need of me, isn't it?"

Carth nodded. "Thank you."

Lindy held her gaze. "You will either save us…"

"Or?"

She hesitated before answering. "Destroy us."

CHAPTER 20

Months had passed since she had last seen Nyaesh. In that time, Carth had become a different person. She had long ago discovered her connection to the shadows, but it was the connection to the S'al that had changed things the most for her. While in Nyaesh and studying with the A'ras, she hadn't managed the same level of skill others possessed. She had power—Invar had seen that about her —but not the easy way to reach it. Since she'd discovered the ability to focus using her mother's ring, even that restriction had changed.

Leaving had been a necessity. She had protected the A'ras from the Hjan, but they had blamed the Reshian. Now they sailed toward Nyaesh only because Carth had no other way of finding the Reshian. Had she had another way, she would have taken it. She didn't want to return to the city.

"You're tense," Dara said.

Carth pulled her attention away from the waves

crashing along the bow of the ship, trying to ignore the sense of growing unease within her, a sense that she suspected came from whatever connection she shared with the city, and looked to where the five survivors of Isahl stood at the railing.

They had passed two empty ships—both Reshian—in their travels toward Nyaesh. How many had the blood priests claimed?

Worse—how powerful had they become?

Even if she managed to convince the A'ras to help— and she wasn't certain she could—there might not be anything they could do against that kind of magic.

"I worry for them in Nyaesh. They don't all know *why* we needed to come."

"There's more to it than that," Dara said.

Carth nodded slowly. "I don't want to return."

"This was your home."

"For a while," Carth answered. "I never really had a home."

"And you blame your father for that."

Carth clenched her jaw. That was the heart of it. Her father had hidden so much from her. Searching for him would provide answers, but was she ready for them? "My father abandoned me."

"You told me that your father ensured you had the training you needed."

"Had I had the training I needed, I would have been better prepared for the Hjan."

Dara laughed softly, and the sound of her voice was drowned out by the crashing of the waves along the ship. "I think you've done well enough, don't you? You defeated them twice in Nyaesh, and then you forced them to make a peace treaty when they wanted old enemies to destroy each other."

Carth smiled. "When you put it like that…" She sighed. "And now there are other worries," she said, looking back to Lindy and Andin.

"Do you really think they could have infiltrated the C'than?"

"I don't know that I understand the C'than, but from what Ras said, I wouldn't put it past them."

"If that's the case, then they would have to have done it long before now."

"And coming to Nyaesh is what we need to do to understand?"

"It's another move," Carth said absently. She hoped she played it right. For this move, at least she knew some of the players and how they would respond. It had been years since she'd known her father, but she *thought* she knew how he would answer. "Perhaps not the one I want, but what we need."

"Want? If I were to have what I wanted, I would have returned to my home, my sisters, and I would have one day married Ril Seaban. Haven't you taught me that we have to play the turn we're given?"

Carth looked over to Dara, realizing that perhaps she'd misjudged the woman. Maybe she *had* been listening during their games. "That's what I've been saying."

"You have. I'm trying to listen."

"I know."

Dara looked over the railing into the distance. "Thank you for your patience. I know I made a mistake…"

"We all do."

"And you've been good about working with me. I appreciate that. I don't know what the slavers would have done with me had you not brought us off the ship."

"You were going to Wesjan either way, I think."

"And you let me do it freely. Just as you should realize that you're doing this freely."

The docks of Nyaesh loomed into view and Carth stared at them, unable to take her eyes off of them. This had been home as much as anything over the years. Now... now her home was this ship.

"Freely, but not by choice. Does that make any sense?" she asked.

"It makes all the sense it needs to make," Dara said.

They fell into silence as the ship slowly approached the shores of Nyaesh. Carth felt a certain heaviness, but also felt pulled toward the shore. She remembered all too well the first time she'd seen Nyaesh, though that had been from the ground. Her parents had never been able to afford boat transport, though it would have been easier to travel. They walked, which Carth now suspected gave them a certain anonymity that traveling by boat would not have allowed.

Guya was a skilled captain and steered them into the docks smoothly. There were dozens of ships docked, more than usual, and Carth saw nothing about them to explain why. Some were familiar and reminded her of the massive ship the blood priests had used, but they had none of the bloodstained sails or hull.

Carth and Dara had grown accustomed to helping tie up when they reached the dock and handled the lines well. Not quite like Guya's previous crew would have managed, but well enough for him not to need to hire others. Learning how to handle the ship had been one stipulation Carth had for him, and Guya had not opposed it. Losing his ship to his first mate had made that an easier decision.

Once settled, Guya met her on the deck. He wore a beige shirt that had little frill to it, yet still had a decorative appearance. A long sword was sheathed at his waist. When Carth cocked her head and nodded to him, he shrugged. "Nyaesh is fancier than some places we've been visiting," he said.

She laughed. "Only fancy if you haven't spent any time here."

"Still fancy," he said.

Dara stood on her other shoulder, hands holding on to the railing. "What do you intend to do?"

"This part of the city is nothing but docks and taverns," Carth said. Her gaze drifted to the Wounded Lyre. She could see the outline of it from where they were situated. After all the time she'd been away, she still felt drawn to it. Were Hal and Vera still even there? Would there be anyone else she knew there?

Yet… most her time in the city had been spent with the A'ras. She had spent countless days within the palace walls, training and hoping for answers.

"That's not where you intend to go," Guya said.

"It's not."

"What of them?" he asked, nodding to those from Isahl. Andin stared at the city, his eyes a mixture of wide-eyed excitement and distrust. Lindy stood observing, one hand planted on her hips, her mouth pinched tightly.

"They should remain on board for now," she said. "The last time I was here, the Reshian weren't well received."

"They're not from Reshian," Dara said.

"No, but they have similar sentiments. I think we're less likely to have trouble with them if they remain on board."

Guya looked from Carth to Dara and shook his head. "Guess I don't get to experience the fancy."

Carth clapped him on the shoulder. It *was* best for him to stay on board, but she didn't want to be the one to suggest it. "I'll make sure you get a chance at some finery."

He grinned at her, then lowered the ramp for them to climb down.

As soon as Carth reached the dock and entered the city, old emotions washed over her. She stopped on the street leading toward the rest of the city, watching the people moving around her, and flashed back to when she'd been younger. As hard as that time had been, they weren't all bad memories.

"This was where I learned to steal," Carth said softly.

"You were a thief?" Dara asked.

They made their way along the street, and Carth made a point of not looking back, and not focusing on the Lyre. "I was a thief, but we never considered ourselves thieves. We were always strays, and the money we took scraps from strangers."

"I imagine with your connection to the shadows, you were skilled at taking scraps."

"More than the others. I didn't have to collect for as long."

They started up the wide Doland Street, which led toward the palace. From here, she considered the old herbalist whom she'd briefly thought she would be able to learn from. Before that woman had disappeared, Carth had hoped she would have been able to work with her, and that she would have been able to learn an honest trade. Even in that, it was not meant to be.

As they crested a rise, there was the glimmer of sunlight off the palace.

Coming into the city this way, first by water and then through the streets, she was more aware than ever of the connection to the A'ras magic. It pulled on her, drawing her forward. She still didn't understand the A'ras flame, but she understood that it was the power that allowed the A'ras to use a magic like what those of Lashasn used.

"You haven't told me where we're heading," Dara said.

Carth noted that she held on to a hint of power. Would the A'ras notice the same, or would the fact that she connected more directly to it prevent them from seeing it? Invar might know, but then Invar was connected in the same way as Carth, and as Dara.

She pointed toward the palace.

"The palace? Who do you know in the palace?"

"That is where the A'ras train," she said.

"First a thief, and then a princess. You've lived quite the life, Carth."

She snorted. "Not a princess." But she was right. Coming to Nyaesh, she *had* lived quite a life. Was it the one her parents had wanted for her? Was this what they had expected when they had brought her here?

She couldn't believe this would be what her mother had wanted for her. Her mother would have wanted her to have peace. Yet… this was where her mother had brought her. They had intended for her to come to Nyaesh, and they had likely intended for her to learn from the A'ras. With that being the case, why should it surprise her that she had ended up here, and done what she had?

Carth had rarely walked along Doland Street so openly. When she had lived with Vera and Hal at the Wounded Lyre, Carth had come this way mostly while chasing others and collecting scraps. When she had lived in the palace, she had come this way when patrolling, but there had never been a time when she'd felt as if she belonged out in the street. There had never been a time when she'd felt safe. Even after training with the A'ras, she hadn't felt safe, not with the potential for both Reshian and Hjan attacks. She had better control of her abilities now and nothing to fear.

She looked around, expecting to find others of the A'ras patrolling, but so far, they hadn't come across anyone. There was no one with the maroon sash. The streets carried a boisterous sort of noise, one that was a sharp contrast to what she'd heard in Isahl, or even what she'd experienced in Odian. This was a vibrancy to the city, one that Carth now recognized as healthy.

Why weren't other cities like this?

"What is it?" Dara asked her.

Carth shook her head. "It's nothing. Just more questions," she said.

They reached the wall surrounding the palace. She could use the shadows or the A'ras magic and leap the wall, but that would get her nowhere. Then she would have to sneak through the grounds, which she had no intention of doing. She needed answers and wanted to come openly so that she could get them.

At the wall, she paused.

Two A'ras stood on either side of the gate, both wearing sheathed long swords, with the maroon sash wrapped around their arms. The nearest was a face she recognized and hadn't expected to see quite so soon upon her return. She had thought it possible that she might see him, but what were the odds that Samis patrolled the gate?

"You know him?" Dara asked.

"I know him."

"That should make it easier."

Carth sighed. "Not exactly."

Taking a deep breath, she approached Samis at the gate.

CHAPTER 21

Carth tried framing what she would say in her mind while making her way toward him. What *was* there to say to Samis? He had been out in the field of Wesjan during the attack, but she hadn't approached. The only one who knew she was there had been Invar, and he hadn't revealed her presence to anyone else. As far as Samis knew, she had last been on the grounds when the Hjan had attacked, and she had betrayed the A'ras.

"The grounds are closed," Samis said. He didn't look at her—not *really* look at her. His hand hovered near the hilt of his sword. She knew him to be a skilled swordsman, and he had defeated her every time they had sparred in the past. But that was before she had discovered the connection to the S'al.

"I would like to see Master Invar."

Samis shook his head. "Invar isn't available." He met her eyes and blinked. His hand gripped his sword with more force. "*Rel?*"

She nodded. "I need to see Invar, Samis."

"Dammit, Rel, you shouldn't have come."

"I had to come."

"The last time you were here, you were the reason the Reshian attacked."

Could he still believe that? How many others did as well?

"Is that what you think? Didn't Alison tell you what I did?"

He shook his head. "Alison… she's not able to tell us anything, Rel."

Carth wondered what had happened to her friend. Alison had talent and skill, but had needed time to develop. With the attack, and with the forced confrontation between the A'ras and the Reshian, she wouldn't have been given the time she needed.

The other A'ras looked over at Carth and Samis. Carth didn't recognize the younger man, surprised that the A'ras would have someone his age standing guard. More had changed than she had realized.

"I need to see Invar," she said again.

"You can't, Rel."

"Why?"

"You don't know what's happened since you left. There was almost a war. We have a peace accord now, but it won't hold. It can't, not when the Reshian are involved. Not when they've been attacking."

Dara looked over to Carth.

Attacking? Was that what the A'ras believed?

Would the Reshian think the same as the A'ras and believe they were responsible? Did the Reshian mistakenly blame the A'ras for attacks made by the blood priests?

Could the Hjan *not* be involved for once?

"I think I understand more than you realize," she said.

"No. We left the city. The A'ras sent hundreds out under the masters' guidance, with the intent to fight the Reshian. It's lucky that we didn't."

"Not luck. And I know that you were in Wesjan."

"You know?"

"I was there too."

The other A'ras stepped closer, and his gaze flickered to her knife. For someone with any knowledge, they would recognize the knife as one of the Reshian.

He slipped his sword from his sheath. "She's with them!" he said, pulling the knife free.

The power of the A'ras flame poured from him. He might be young, but he was strong as well. She understood why he would be allowed to patrol.

He raised his sword and readied an attack, slicing toward her without any additional warning.

Carth pushed Dara back with a surge of shadows and slipped her knife free from her sheath, drawing only on her A'ras magic as she did. If she used the shadows, she would be the very thing that he accused her of being.

She caught his sword with the flat of her knife and twisted it, forcing it down.

He pulled on more of the A'ras magic. To her, it was a burning sensation beneath her skin, a familiar sense that she hadn't detected with quite as much regularity since she'd left here. She knew it when Dara used her magic, but the connection was different. Dara connected to the

S'al in a purer sense, nothing like the way the most of the A'ras could reach the flame.

With a quick twist, he freed his sword and swung around again.

Carth caught him again, this time sending a surge of S'al through the knife. It wasn't the same type of blade she would have made were she to have remained here, but there was still power that flowed through it, and it sent a flash as she did.

The boy took a step back and blinked.

"You're A'ras?"

"Was," Samis said, looking at Carth with a strange expression. "She *was* A'ras. Go find if Invar can see her. Tell them Carthenne Rel is here to see Invar."

"You know that Invar can't take visitors—"

Samis shook his head. "Go."

"What of you?"

"I was always able to stop Rel before."

Carth smiled at the memory. At the time, there wouldn't have been a smile. She had hated the way that Samis had always managed to defeat her, a result of her strange delay with the A'ras magic. Now that she wore her mother's ring, she suspected the outcome would be different, though she didn't really want to test it with him.

When the boy had disappeared, Samis nodded to her knife. "It seems you've gotten quicker with your abilities," he said.

"My mother," she started, before cutting herself off. Would he know about Ih and Lashasn? Would he care? Would it matter if he did?

She decided it didn't.

"That doesn't make any sense."

"My mother was Lashasn. I have some of her abilities."

He frowned. "If you say so. You were there, then?"

"Wesjan?"

He nodded. "Invar disappeared, and when he came back to us, he said he'd found an old friend who would help end the war. No one believed him until the treaty was signed. I don't think anyone wanted to fight the Reshian like that. We'd already faced too much, and had lost too much before then."

"That was the Hjan," she said. "They were trying to coordinate the war. They wanted you to destroy each other."

He sighed. "I don't know if they did or not, but it very nearly worked. You were there when the treaty was signed?"

"I'm the reason the treaty was signed."

Samis just nodded.

They stood in silence for a while, and Dara didn't say anything either. Carth wondered how long it would take for Invar to come and if the boy would even be able to find him. If he couldn't, then it wouldn't have mattered that Carth had come to the city. Speaking to Samis was nice, but she would learn nothing from Samis; she would only feel the same confusion she had felt when she had been in the A'ras.

She didn't know how long passed with them staring at each other when she felt A'ras magic used near her. There was a signature to it, and this one she recognized before it faded.

The A'ras who had been at the gate came running back. When he reached Samis, he shook his head.

Samis studied her. "Sorry, Rel. Looks like Invar can't see you."

"That's it?"

Samis shrugged. "That's it. You're not A'ras. Whatever you are… it's something else."

"Samis—"

"You shouldn't have returned, Rel. There's nothing for you here."

CHAPTER 22

Carth led Dara away from the palace and around the wall, avoiding the gates. It made her feel all too much like the uncertain girl who had once attempted to sneak into the palace. That had been before she knew about the A'ras, and before she knew about her shadows, and before she knew about anything. Her life had been so much simpler then.

"What do you intend to do?" Dara asked.

Guya remained on the ship, waiting for them. Carth fully expected a need to pull out of the harbor quickly, which meant they would have to set sail as soon as they returned. Andin would help; together they could use the shadows to drive the ship from the harbor and out into the river. From there, they would use the currents and the power of the river to help them make the rest of the journey.

"I need to see Invar. We need allies against the blood priests."

And there was something off about what Samis said, though she couldn't put her finger on it. Was Invar in trouble?

"You think they'll ally with you?"

Carth sighed. "Maybe not with me, but Invar will see what happened. He'll understand." He had to. She had to reach him.

"How?"

"First, we have to clear the wall," she said.

"You sound like you think that might be difficult."

Carth sighed. "Crossing the wall won't be the most difficult. I can use the shadows for that. But once we're on the other side of the wall, my shadow ability will be neutralized. The wall has power embedded into it that defeats the shadows."

"How? Why?"

"When I was here, I hadn't learned enough to ask the questions that you do. I should have, but I hadn't considered *why* we wouldn't be able to use the shadows. Why would the A'ras specifically close out the shadow abilities? It took me too long to realize that there has long been animosity between Lashasn and Ih."

"They can stop the Reshian from using their abilities?"

Carth took a deep breath as she ran her hand along the wall. This section was one of the rebuilt sections from the attack. The stone was different, and she knew that the ivy on the other side of the wall would be different as well. If she could cross here, she would still be able to hold on to the shadows, maybe enough to do what she needed to do.

"There was a man who taught me that it was possible."

"Do you know how?"

Carth shook her head. "I know that it's possible. I suppose that's enough to know. Once you know something can be done, it becomes easier to do." She pulled her hand away from the wall. "Are you ready?"

Dara nodded. "As much as I can be."

Carth took her hand and pulled on the shadows, drawing them around her as tightly as she could. She felt them fill her, practically spraying from her. And then she jumped.

Holding on to Dara made the jump more difficult, but not impossible. It carried her up and over the wall, and she landed on the grass on the other side. Still holding on to the shadows, she shielded them, keeping hidden. It didn't work for her to flow with the shadows, to move the way she had once been taught to move. She wasn't strong enough on this side of the wall to do it with more than herself. Even if she only tried doing it with herself, she might not have been strong enough.

Carth released the shadows, holding her connection to them, not wanting to lose it altogether. She hurried to a copse of trees and looked around.

"What do you detect?" she asked Dara.

She didn't feel the sense of burning, nothing that would indicate that there were A'ras using their abilities nearby, but that didn't mean they weren't here. With her holding on to the shadows, she didn't know if she would detect it well.

"There's a faint sense, but it's out there," she said, pointing through the trees and toward the spire of the palace, which was only barely visible.

Of course, that would be where they would detect it.

She suspected the palace contained other protections that would prevent her from using the shadows. She could use the A'ras magic, but here everyone she might encounter would be able to do the same.

"I don't know if it will be safe for you to come with me," she told Dara.

"Safe? When have we ever done anything that's safe?"

Carth shook her head. "This isn't something to joke about. If we're caught… I know what they'll do to me," she started, trying not to think about the violence she might encounter from people who had once been friends, "but with your ability, they might hold you, and would want to use you."

Dara clenched her jaw. "I'm bound with you in this, Carth. I know I made a mistake—"

Carth shook her head. "This isn't about that at all."

"Then let me help. Let's do this together. Besides, didn't you say they would teach me?"

She hoped the A'ras would teach, but without reaching Invar, she wasn't certain she could trust what they would do. He was the only A'ras *she* trusted.

Carth met Dara's gaze and held it for long moment. She noted the determination behind Dara's eyes and knew she had to find a way to work with her. This was what she'd wanted for Dara, wasn't it? A chance for her to learn from the A'ras? If Carth could find a way to understand what had happened, maybe she'd be able to find someone for Dara to work with. Maybe Carth could understand what had happened with her friends.

Carth slipped her knife from the sheath and started forward. As she did, she held on to her link to the shadows, but that grew more and more difficult the further she went. By the time the palace was fully in view, she had lost her connection altogether.

Carth breathed out, sending a connection through the ring as she reached for the power of the S'al. It amazed her that the key to the connection had been with her from the moment she had begun studying with the A'ras, and she hadn't discovered it until she'd run away, thinking to hone the skills she'd developed with the Reshian.

Now, with her mother's ring, she was somehow better able to reach for that part of her that could use the S'al, as if it unlocked something inside her so that the delay she'd felt while working with the A'ras, the delay that had limited her and caused her to take so long moving to ashai, was no more. Now she reached it smoothly and quickly, nearly with the same efficiency as when she reached for the shadow magic.

Here, within the palace yard, there was no restriction on the A'ras magic. It filled her now in ways that it never had when she had studied here. She let it wash over her and wondered if she glowed the way that Dara seemed to glow when she used her abilities.

Wrapped in the A'ras magic as she was, she felt the subtle use of it within the palace. There were several places where she detected it, some stronger than others. One was the strongest of all. That was where they had to go.

Carth nodded to Dara. "Follow closely. Maintain your connection to the power. I think that if you don't, we could be separated from it."

Dara's eyes widened slightly, and she nodded.

Carth reached a side door and noted the two A'ras standing guard.

She flashed forward, attacking with the flat of her knife before either of them could even react. Both fell, dropping wordlessly to the ground.

"Help me drag them inside."

Dara grabbed the smaller of the two, and they pushed the door open, carrying the A'ras. They didn't see anyone else, but Carth hadn't expected to see anyone else here. Each time she'd come before, she had found the hall empty.

"Where now?" Dara asked.

Carth focused on what she felt of the A'ras magic. It flared all around her, but there wasn't anything that she could detect.

Would she be able to detect the shadows now that she was this far into the A'ras compound?

She felt their pull, but it was fainter than it had been near the wall, and Carth didn't know if she would even be able to use it for so much as a shadow cloak, let alone anything more substantial.

There was a noise in the hall that told her they weren't going to be alone for much longer. Stranger still was the steady pulsing of A'ras magic against her, a tapping that she thought had something like a pattern, one that was familiar for some reason, as if she had sensed it before.

Because she had.

"Invar," she whispered.

Carth started down the hall, searching for Invar, but knowing where she would be likely to find him. Why would he signal her this way? She wasn't surprised that he'd detected her. He had the same connection to the S'al that she did, the same connection that allowed her the ability to detect when others used it. Invar could detect it just as well. Better, she suspected. He'd been using the A'ras magic for far longer than her.

She reached the end of a hall that she had last visited the day she had left Nyaesh. As she did, footsteps stormed up behind her. Carth spun and found Samis approaching.

"Rel. You shouldn't have breached the wall."

"I only need to see Invar."

"I told you the answer."

"Yes. You did. *He* didn't."

"If you think to challenge me, Rel, you'll find I'm better equipped than the last time."

"Not challenge. I intend to speak to Invar."

"You don't get to make that choice—"

He cut off as the door opened, and Invar stood watching, his gaze bouncing from her to Samis, then settling on Dara.

Invar had always been powerful. From the very first time she'd met him, and then from when she'd worked with him, she had known him to have exquisite control. It was the kind of control she had wished she could learn with the A'ras magic, and the kind of control Dara would need to learn. Carth had managed only a fraction of what he'd demonstrated, and though she had attempted to continue her practice, the power and knowledge she possessed was nothing compared to what Invar was capable of.

His magic pulsed, and she knew it to be something of a

demonstration for her, a way for her to know that he was here.

Carth pulsed back.

The effect was slight, barely a touch of the power, but with Invar, it was enough for him to know what she did.

"Ms. Rel," he said. "You have gained a subtler control, haven't you?"

"I've tried to learn what I can," she said.

"And you seem to have learned quite a bit." His eyes noted her mother's ring and widened slightly. Had Invar recognized it? Had she only worn it during her time with the A'ras, she would have managed to reach that power more easily. It had been a mistake not even trying it, but how was she to know that her mother must have possessed the power of the Lashasn?

"I haven't learned anything," she said. "But that's why I'm here."

Invar tipped his head and shot a warning gaze toward Samis before settling once more on Carth. "Why *are* you here, Ms. Rel? You were sent from the city, I seem to recall."

He pulsed his power again.

"I came to remove her, Invar," Samis said.

Carth realized what troubled her. Samis continued to refer to him as *Invar*, not *Master* Invar.

What had happened here?

"I can manage well enough," Invar said, sending a subtle pulse.

This was even lighter than before, and he did it in such a way that Carth had to think it a warning. Why would

Invar need to warn her? What was there that he would need to warn against?

"I…" She hesitated as she tried to think of why she would have come here, trying to think of a good reason and one that, if Invar's warning was real, she would be able to downplay. Could it be about Samis? That didn't seem right. That meant there was another reason.

What would she be able to tell him that would justify her return to the city without exposing those she'd found in Isahl?

The answer was with her.

Carth hoped Dara understood.

"I brought someone with A'ras ability to learn," she said.

Invar glanced beyond Carth and looked to Dara. Carth nodded to her friend and hoped that she would understand. They could have Dara pretend, and then they would get her free. She wouldn't have to stay.

"Such a thing is unconventional," Invar said.

"So was I."

"That is my concern."

Carth sighed. If only there were an easier answer, but until she knew what was going on, she needed to be cautious. Then she could find out what had happened. "Dara is more skilled than I was when Avera brought me to the A'ras. Give her a chance."

Invar studied Dara, and power built, this time from Samis, a power that settled over Dara before fading.

Carth frowned. Why would Samis use his ability on her to test her? That was something the masters would do, and Samis would have a long way to go before he was one of the masters.

"You may go," Invar said to Samis. "Unless you think I will cause trouble within the hall?" Samis frowned. "You know Carthenne, Samis. Do not pretend that you do not. You were her friend. Whatever has happened since then… you were her friend. You would do well to remember that, especially considering what else you might think to do."

Carth wasn't sure what Samis might do. If he was against Invar, would he betray her to whatever A'ras were displeased with the accords?

Samis said nothing and hurried away.

Invar watched him go before turning to Carth. "Come inside, Ms. Rel. We have much to speak about."

CHAPTER 23

CARTH SAT INSIDE THE MASTER HALL FOR THE FIRST TIME in over a year. As soon as they had entered the room, Invar had sealed it with a wave of his hand, creating a barrier of power that Carth could feel but few others would have been able to detect. The room looked little different than the last time Carth had been here. Then, shelves cluttered with books had lined the walls. That was still the case, but there were fewer than there once had been. The long table that had once occupied much of the center of the room was gone, replaced by three chairs, all angled toward each other. The basin with the flame burning in it was unchanged. Carth could feel the sense of the flame pulling on her, an awareness of the magic that she'd felt from the very first time she'd come here.

"Now. Why are you really here?" Invar asked.

"What's going on? Why the charade?"

Invar swept his hand around the room. "There are

some who are displeased with the alliance. They blame me for the accords."

"Blame you?"

He nodded. "They would prefer that we remain in conflict with the Reshian."

"But the Hjan—"

"I understand why we fought, Ms. Rel. You don't have to explain it to me."

"What of the other masters?"

Invar frowned and took a seat. "Others? There are none, Ms. Rel. There is me, and that is it. After the attack on the city, we had so few of us remaining. No others have been raised. And now I am not allowed out of this room."

"You could—"

"Could what? Fight the A'ras, Ms. Rel? We need peace, and it will not do for us to fracture internally. We have been through enough as it is."

"Was that why Samis acted the way that he did?"

"Samis has grown more skilled. He is competent, I won't take that away from him, but he is still young. And with youth comes a belief that you know better than you do."

Carth smiled. "I'm young."

"And you have made the same sorts of mistakes." He motioned for her to sit. When she did, he sighed. "You saw the end of the battle, and for that, I think, you deserve thanks. You will never get it, and you will never be known as the architect of the accords, but you should."

"I don't want the recognition," Carth said. "That wasn't why I did it."

"No. I know that it is not."

They sat in silence. The flame crackled occasionally, but it had a supernatural sound to it, almost a sighing sort of sound. There wasn't the steady hiss of a lantern burning with oil, and there was nothing of the crackling of logs in a hearth. This was almost a hiss, almost a voice, and Carth wondered if she could understand it.

"Do you know how to find the Reshian?" Carth asked after it became apparent that he wasn't going to say anything more.

"Why do you think I would know how to find the Reshian?"

"Because I know you, Invar. I know that you would have some way of reaching them."

"Why do you need to reach them?"

"I returned to Ih-lash."

"As you should. You are a child of Ih-lash."

Carth stared at the flame. It was connected to the Lashasn ability in some way, but what was it? That was a question that had always troubled her.

But if there was a flame that allowed the A'ras to reach the Lashasn magic, was there something similar for the Ih magic? Was there something that would let others reach the shadows?

The flame had been the reason the Hjan had come here and attacked in the palace, hadn't it? They had wanted to extinguish the flame, and destroy the A'ras connection to it. If they had succeeded, almost all the A'ras would have lost their power, and they would have no longer been able to protect Nyaesh. The Hjan would have managed to invade.

Not only the Hjan, but wouldn't the Reshian have been able to do the same?

Only, they had managed to protect the flame. Invar had relit it, so that the flame allowed those of the A'ras to continue using their magic. Had he not, Nyaesh would have fallen.

Carth realized what it was that bothered her.

Ih-lash had fallen, and there had been those with the ability to use the shadows. Had they possessed an ability like the A'ras to have their flame and pass those abilities on to others who would not have otherwise possessed them, why couldn't Ih have had something similar with the shadows?

She stood. It was a question she needed to ask of the refugees from Isahl.

"What is it, Ms. Rel?"

"I need to find the Reshian," she said again.

"I believe you have shared that with me already."

"They're in danger. And the A'ras might be the only ones able to help. That's why I'm here. If you can't help—"

"You will find the A'ras unwilling to make such a commitment," Invar said.

"It's important."

"I'm certain that it is, just as I'm certain that the Reshian—or Ih—and Lashasn have fought for hundreds of years. Your accords would do nothing but slow it—they would not stop it."

Carth studied him, thinking that he might say something more. "Do you know anything about practitioners of a blood magic?"

His eyes narrowed. "A foul thing."

"Yes. They hunt the Reshian. The flame can defeat them. That's why I'm here."

Invar sighed. "As I said, Ms. Rel, there has been fighting between the Reshian and Lashasn for many years. The accords will not change that."

"And others will?"

"Possibly."

"Like the C'than?"

The corner of his mouth twitched. "Ras told you."

"He didn't have to. Could the Hjan infiltrate the C'than?"

"Doubtful."

"But possible."

"Is that why you have come, Ms. Rel?"

"I told you why I returned."

"And I told you my answer. Perhaps you would be interested in training."

"I think I've trained enough."

"All of us could use a little more."

Carth grinned at the suggestion, imagining Invar receiving additional training. "Even you?"

"Even me, Ms. Rel."

She turned to the flame, troubled by the idea of Ih and those who could use the shadows having something similar. "You don't know where to find the Reshian?"

"That is not what I said."

"So you do?" She turned toward Invar, frowning at him.

"Why would you find them?" he asked.

"My father is with them."

Invar pressed the tips of his fingers together, looking

up at her through lids that seemed heavy. "When did you discover this?"

"You knew." It wasn't even a question. The way he said it made it clear to her that he did. And if Invar had known, why hadn't he shared with her?

"I knew that your father still lived. Had you been willing to think through what you had seen, you would have known as well."

Carth grunted. "You sound like Ras."

"Ras is wise."

She didn't know whether to call Ras wise, but he certainly had taught her to see things in a different way. Without his training, she would never have begun to look at the world from different perspectives. She needed to continue doing it, but it required her to understand things that she didn't know. Information continued to be a challenge for her, and it frustrated her.

"Where are they?"

"The C'than are interested in maintaining the accords."

"I thought you said they didn't matter."

"I said the Reshian and Lashasn had fought for many years."

"That's not an answer."

"No, but it is all I can give."

"Even if someone from the Reshian is working with the Hjan?"

"I find that unlikely."

Was it unlikely?

Everything seemed to be a game within a game, and somehow she had to sort it out, only she wasn't certain that she knew enough about the players.

Maybe there *wasn't* any infiltration to the C'than, only that the Hjan wanted them to believe it.

Perhaps it was time for her to take on a greater role.

First, she needed answers.

"What happened to Alison?"

Invar took a deep breath. "I have told you that there are those who would rather see the accords severed. There are those who feel otherwise. Alison does not believe we should violate them. The others are displeased."

"What does that mean?"

"You will find her better protected than I. At least I have some freedoms. That comes from my previous station. Alison... she is less comfortable."

Carth took a deep breath, testing her connection to the shadows. They were there. It was faint, but they were there.

With her mother's ring, the connection to the A'ras magic was even stronger. "When do they plan to attack?" That would be the only reason for them to confine Invar to his room, and to confine Alison as well. It would explain why she had seen no other A'ras on the street. It would explain why she had been challenged when she'd arrived at the gate.

"Now you begin to ask the right questions."

"When?"

She thought about the ships she'd seen when they had docked. Now it made sense. They were battleships, readying for an assault on the Reshian, which meant someone knew where to find them.

Before Invar could answer, someone started banging on the door.

Invar looked to her. "I'm sorry, Ms. Rel. You should not have returned. I think you will be able to get yourself free, but I don't know about the other."

The door burst open. Six A'ras stood on the other side, each with a wide sash of their stations around their wrists or forearms. All had their swords unsheathed and slowly started to enter the room.

"You were with them," the nearest said. She remembered him as Evan, a boy who had always been kind to her, but now he looked at her with violence in his eyes.

"Leave, Ms. Rel, or you will likely suffer," Master Invar said.

Evan shot Invar a glare. "You have always deceived us. First with the Reshian attack and then with the treaty. *They* haven't abided by the treaty, so we will not either."

Carth realized that bringing Andin and the others from Isahl had been a mistake. If the A'ras discovered them, they would harm them and it would be her fault, all because she had wanted to help them, and had believed that she could for some reason.

There came the slow burn of fire along her arms. Power built and it came from each of the A'ras. Not Master Invar. He didn't resist, and Carth wondered why he didn't.

"You should leave, Ms. Rel."

"She's not leaving. Now that she's here—"

Carth didn't want to attack them and hurt them, and she realized that she might not have to. There was another way to stop them, at least to slow them. They would still be skilled with the sword without their magic.

She turned to the flame.

With a pulse of shadow, she extinguished it.

It went out with a huff of smoke.

Invar gasped and said, "Oh."

Carth turned back to the A'ras. "You will find the odds decidedly more in my favor now," she told them. "Retreat now and I will let you live."

CHAPTER 24

W‍HEN THE FIRST ATTACK CAME, C‍ARTH WAS READY.

She unsheathed her knife and, pulling the A'ras magic through both the knife and the ring, she pressed out.

The nearest A'ras—one she didn't recognize—came at her with his sword drawn. Carth noted the attack and countered easily. In the time she'd been gone from A'ras, she'd continued to work with the sword. The A'ras were skilled, but there were other blade masters in the world, and she had incorporated their techniques into what she did. In that way, she fought more like she played Tsatsun, thinking ahead, planning for the next strike and preparing herself for what it might be.

The knife offered some advantages the sword didn't have. There was less reach, but she was quicker, and in the confined space and with the shadows on her side, she didn't need the reach.

Carth flowed forward.

She had to incapacitate and not kill. Somehow, that would have to be the outcome.

Using the S'al wouldn't work here. She would have to use the shadows.

Doing so pitted her against the A'ras. It would make them believe the Reshian had attacked again. It might violate the accords, but hadn't they already done that?

She needed answers so that they could stop the blood priests. More than that, they needed allies. Using the shadows would pit the A'ras against the Reshian.

Carth swore under her breath. For that reason, she *couldn't* use the shadows.

Taking a deep breath, she pulled on the power of the S'al.

As she did, the flame in the bowl flared into existence, a flash of light so bright it was blinding.

Carth glanced back to it, wondering if it was what she did or something that Invar had done.

He shook his head.

Not Invar.

Two A'ras attacked.

She flipped the sword of the first attacker toward the ground and kicked, catching him in the chest. For the second, she spun, flicking his feet from beneath him and leaving him on the ground. She made a point of kicking him in the temple, not hard enough to kill but enough to knock him out.

That left four of the A'ras.

The space was narrow enough they couldn't all attack at once. If they did, she'd have no choice and would have to use the shadows. At least this way, she could take them on one on one.

When she'd been in Nyaesh and studying in the palace, she hadn't been more skilled than anyone else. Her ability and connection to the shadows made the difference for her. Since leaving, she'd discovered a greater connection to the S'al magic and had taken the time to continue to improve with the sword.

It still wasn't enough.

She recognized the next A'ras as he attacked. Tern had been full A'ras the entire time she'd been ashai, and he was rumored to be incredibly skilled. Seeing the way he fought, she believed it.

His blade was a fury, and it moved so quickly that even the other three A'ras gave him space. Behind him, Evan watched with a hint of a grin. Now that the flame had surged forth again, they used their A'ras magic against her as well, powering their attack.

"I could use your help, Invar."

"If I help…"

She understood. If he helped her, he committed to abandoning the A'ras.

She couldn't have him do that, but she needed to get free from here without hurting anyone too badly—and without using her shadows.

Light exploded from behind Evan.

He spun.

The other A'ras hesitated.

Carth used that moment to attack, sending her knife in a tight arc as she sliced toward them. She caught him in the shoulder and he dropped the sword. Carth kicked, sending him flying backward and into two of the other A'ras.

Another surge of light hit her.

Carth darted forward, and into the remaining A'ras. Throwing an elbow, she knocked one of them down and then caught Tern with her knee, doubling him over so she could slam the hilt of her knife into the back of his head. He crumpled.

That left Evan.

He flicked his gaze from side to side. There was another surge of A'ras magic, enough that Carth was briefly blinded. It struck Evan, and then he disappeared.

Carth used a hint of the shadows, barely more than a trickle, and pushed out, clearing her vision.

When she did, she saw Samis standing opposite her. Alison was with him. Both carried swords, unsheathed.

"Carth?" Alison asked, sheathing her sword. "What are you doing here?"

She glanced from Samis back to Alison, trying to understand what she might have missed. "I would ask you the same thing."

"They accused me of working with—"

"The Reshian?" Carth finished.

Alison nodded, glancing carefully toward Samis. "You shouldn't be here. With your abilities, you're only going to incite a violation of the treaty."

"They've already violated the treaty," Samis said. "Why do you think we've been so active?"

"The Reshian wouldn't have violated the accords," Carth said.

"How would you know?" Alison asked.

"Because they don't want to fight the A'ras any more than the A'ras want to fight them. They're trying to stay alive."

"What?"

"The Reshian face a different threat than the A'ras or the Hjan. And they're in much more danger than the A'ras. That's why I'm here. They don't know it, but the Reshian need your help."

Invar ran his hand along the inside of the flame. She expected him to get burned, but when he pulled his hand away, it was unharmed.

"What you did there was impressive," he said, nodding toward the flame.

"Extinguishing it? That's just a matter of using the shadows."

Invar smiled. "Not the extinguishing of the flame. The rekindling of it." He glanced to her hand, noting the ring she wore. "Working together to light the flame is difficult enough. There are few with the strength to light it alone. You really have grown stronger since we last met."

"I've been forced to, Invar. Everywhere I've gone, I've been used."

"You were never used here."

Carth tipped her head. "No? I think my parents even intended for me to be used by the A'ras. My mother was Lashasn, and she wanted me to come here to develop my abilities."

"That is different than getting used."

"How? I was here because I descend from both Lashasn and Ih. I can use the abilities of both ancient bloodlines. That fact was used to stop the war."

"I would argue that you did something necessary."

"It doesn't change that I've been used." She fixed him with a hard gaze. "Will you help?"

"I don't know that I can."

"Because you aren't willing to, or you're afraid?" she asked.

"I've told you—"

"Yes. The Reshian and Lashasn have been in conflict for centuries."

"The accords will only delay it for a moment."

"Then the Hjan will attack," Carth said. Invar nodded. "We can stop it, Invar. *You* can help stop it."

As she left, Invar said, "You will always be welcome in Nyaesh, Ms. Rel."

Carth paused at the door. "I was never welcome in Nyaesh."

As she passed through the doorway, she fixed Alison and Samis with a gaze. "You can come with me if you'd like."

"What are you going to do?" Alison asked.

Carth glanced back to Invar. He watched her as well, his hand resting on the basin holding the flame. She should remain in Nyaesh and find out more about the flame, learn why it was that she could reach the S'al completely while others needed to draw from the flame of the A'ras, but what did it matter? In that sense, she was born to the S'al no differently than she was born to the shadows. The others… they were more like the shadow blessed. Able to touch the basic ability, but nothing more.

She sighed. What would she do?

She had been used, but even she understood that it had

been necessary. Her parents had brought her to Nyaesh in hopes of finding peace. And she *had* forged it. Because of her, the accords were in place. Now she had to see that they remained.

That meant understanding and knowledge. That meant that she was not surprised. That meant that she had the pieces of her board arranged in such a way that others would not be able to outmaneuver her.

Carth didn't know how she would do it, but she would have to find a way.

Alison watched her, her eyes filled with unasked questions.

"I will do what is needed."

"And that is?" This came from Samis. Some of the doubt he'd displayed had eased, and now he watched her as carefully as Invar.

"I intend to see that peace remains."

CHAPTER 25

THE DOCKS ALONG THE RIVER ROAD REMAINED AS BUSY AS
Carth remembered. The scents here were the same—that
of fish and a hint of salt from the distant sea and the
promise of rain. Noise filled the air, that of gulls cawing
and hawkers yelling and children playfully running
through the street. Carth knew enough to watch the children in particular. If anyone would be likely to sneak up
and attempt to steal from her, it would be the children.

Carth noted the *Spald* and the fact that it didn't seem
to be in any danger before turning away and heading
down the street.

"Carth?" Alison asked.

She turned. Samis had remained on the palace
grounds. Carth hadn't actually expected him to join her,
but it would have been nice having another friend with
her, even if the connection she'd forged with him had
changed when he'd betrayed her. With Alison, there was
history between them, but it didn't feel as easy or as

comfortable as it once had. Still, Alison had agreed to come. In many ways, Carth wasn't surprised.

"Where are you going?" Alison glanced to Dara, but Dara only shrugged.

Carth nodded to the solitary building at the intersection of River Road. It was a low-roofed wooden building with shuttered windows and a plain-looking door that was tightly closed. A faded sign hung from a hook off the front. Carth didn't need to see the sign to recognize the sigil.

"There's one stop I have to make," she said.

Alison nodded and fell silent.

Carth approached the Wounded Lyre as she would approach an attacker: with uncertainty and a hint of anxiety. Just like with an attacker, she didn't exactly feel fear, but there was enough worry that gnawed in her belly that she wasn't comfortable either.

Years had passed since she'd come.

When she'd been freed to patrol the city, she'd almost stopped here several times. Why hadn't she? Was it because she was afraid of what she'd find, or was it because she was afraid she wouldn't have been missed? Maybe it was a combination of both. The Lyre had been a place of safety to her when she'd badly needed it, and then had become a place where *she* was the liability. Her presence had put the others in danger. Leaving had been the only way to keep them safe, but she'd left without so much as a goodbye.

"I've always wondered what they thought of me," she said as Alison stopped next to her.

"I'm sure they feel the same as they did then."

"Do they? I don't know how they felt then, only that I was welcomed. I was provided for. And I left them." In that way, was she any different to her father? Hadn't he left her when he thought she would be safer without him?

"Are you going to go in?"

She had thought she would. That had been the reason for coming here. But now that she was standing in front of the doorway, Carth wasn't so sure she could. What would she say? What did she hope to accomplish? Going into the Lyre now after all this time wouldn't help her meet any of her objectives. It wouldn't help her understand what had happened with the Reshian, or where her father had gone, or why the blood priests had attacked.

"Sometimes you should allow yourself a chance to feel," Dara said.

Carth sighed. She'd been trained to avoid her feelings. Working with the A'ras, she'd been taught to fight and to get stronger. And then when she'd left, thinking that she'd gone to train with the Reshian, she had learned from Ras to think critically. Emotion hadn't played a part in it other than for her to use her awareness of it to ensure she knew how others would react. Now she didn't even know how *she* would react.

"Going in here won't help me with anything."

"Are you sure?" Dara asked.

Carth watched the door, thinking of all the times she'd run through it. As strange as it was, she had fond memories of her time at the tavern. Vera and Hal had been kind to her, and that kindness had mattered. It still mattered.

"Go," Dara urged.

Carth touched the door.

The shadows shifted.

She felt them flicker. The effect was faint, but it was there.

Carth spun.

"Carth—" Dara started.

She ignored her. The shifting of the shadows came from near the *Spald*.

Carth reached for her knife.

"What is it?" Alison asked, unsheathing her sword.

She shook her head. "I don't know. Something isn't quite right." She didn't know what it was, only that what she felt was wrong. It was more than only the shadows having changed. There was something within the shadows that was wrong.

She started flowing forward, using the shadows as she did, ignoring Alison and Dara's cries for her to wait. How could she wait when she didn't know what was happening? How could she wait when the shadows were off?

There was only one person who she thought could use the shadows like that, but why would Andin do so? She had warned him against it here, and had warned him that Nyaesh would be dangerous for him were he to reveal himself, but Andin hadn't listened. If the A'ras discovered they were here—especially if there were those in the palace inclined to violate the accords...

She knew what would happen. Peace would fail. They would fail. The Hjan would be free to attack again. And too many would suffer.

She reached the ramp leading up onto the *Spald*.

Carth expected to see Guya and the others from Isahl, but they were gone. Had they ventured into the city? Had they been captured? The A'ras were trained and they would be deadly, even against someone like Andin with his ability to use the shadows. The A'ras had experience in stopping those with shadow abilities, and with the previous attacks on the city, she doubted they would handle them lightly.

The deck was empty.

That wasn't completely true. She found a pool of blood near one of the rails and realized that it led over the edge of the ship. Carth looked down and saw a bloodied face bobbing in the water.

Guya.

Carth dove.

She reached Guya quickly and grabbed him under his arms. She was a strong swimmer—more so when she used the shadows to augment her abilities—but the river had a powerful current. It wasn't the first time she'd swum in this river, and each time, it seemed someone's life was in danger. It wasn't even the first time she'd had to swim Guya back to shore. At least this time the shore was closer, though he seemed in worse shape than before.

When she flopped him onto the rocky shore, he coughed and opened his eyes. "Too much like the last time."

"The last time you had a mutiny."

He coughed again and started to sit up. Carth restrained him with a hand to his chest. "No mutiny this time, but an attack."

"The A'ras?"

"Not A'ras."

"The Reshian?" She couldn't imagine Andin attacking

Guya. He had been through quite a bit, but that didn't seem like the kind of thing she would have expected.

"Not the Reshian. They were the ones attacked."

Dara had reached them and, seeing Guya, she touched his head, her skin glowing softly. Dara had some way of healing using the S'al, a trick Carth hadn't taken the time to master. She'd learned that she was protected in some ways—when she'd broken her leg, she had discovered that she healed faster than most—but she hadn't learned to project it outward, not the way that Dara could. Was it something Invar would have taught her had she remained?

Guya gasped, and the bleeding from his scalp slowed.

Dara pulled her hand away. "That's all I can do for now."

"What was *that*?" Alison asked her.

Carth helped Guya to stand. "Dara is Lashasn."

Alison frowned. "Am I supposed to know what that means?"

"You're supposed to know that all of the A'ras originally came from Lashasn. They don't teach that, but it's true. It's like the Reshian and how they come from Ih."

"Ih? As in Ih-lash?"

Carth nodded curtly, eyes scanning the street. The crowd of people who had been out only moments before had disappeared, almost as if they had detected the shifting current of power, but that shouldn't have been possible, not with the shadows used. Had they detected the use of the A'ras magic?

She didn't know. "Do you know where they went?"

"Carth—"

She shot Alison a hard look, cutting her off.

"We need to find them. We need to know where they would have been taken."

Guya wiped his hands on his pants and looked up to his ship. "There were men and one woman. They moved so quietly that I couldn't hear them. When they reached the deck of the ship, they attacked before I even saw them. It was like—"

"They were cloaked in shadows," she finished for him. What he described sounded too much like the movements of someone with a shadow blessing, but why would they have attacked the children of Isahl? Those were their people. They shouldn't have attacked.

"Not shadows," Guya said. "This was something natural. They were quiet, but they weren't magic."

"No abilities?"

"They were unpowered."

Unpowered. The term amused her, but partly because she had once been unpowered, or at least thought herself unpowered. "Then how would they have escaped? If they were unpowered, they would not have been able to disappear easily."

"Carth."

She looked up at Dara and frowned. "Did you see something?"

"Not see. I feel it. Like a soft burning that settled beneath my skin. I… I don't know what it is."

Alison looked from Carth to Dara.

Carth knew what it was that she felt. It was the same thing Carth felt when one of the A'ras used their abilities, something that she never felt outside the city. It came as no surprise that Dara should feel it. Most of the A'ras would not—could not—because they weren't connected as deeply to the S'al as she was, or as deeply as Dara was, but then most weren't as directly descended from the Lashasn as they were either.

"Where?" she asked, but she didn't need to. All she had to do was release her connection to the shadows and she would be able to feel the slow burn of the A'ras power again. As she did, and as she felt it, she recognized where it came from, and recognized the strange shifting of shadows within it as well.

The palace.

And if that was where she detected the shadows, that meant the A'ras now had the Reshian. But Guya hadn't detected the A'ras.

What was going on here?

Regardless of what it was, Carth couldn't leave them. Which meant she would now have to break them out.

CHAPTER 26

THE INSIDE OF THE PALACE YARD WAS QUIET. CARTH thought maybe it was too quiet, but perhaps that was only because she felt on edge after the attack. They had to reach the Reshian and then get out of the palace grounds before getting caught again. When she jumped the fence again, she was met by Invar and Samis.

"I sensed what happened."

"Then you know I couldn't leave them."

"I understand."

"What has happened here?"

"There are those who have taken to actively trying to break the accords, Ms. Rel. I haven't been able to find out how before now, but I fear your blood priests might be allies of theirs."

"Of others in the A'ras? People have died, Invar. Innocents, not only the Reshian." Invar didn't say anything. "Where would they have brought them?"

Samis looked from her to Invar, questions on his face,

but he didn't say anything. Carth was thankful that he'd helped, but still didn't know whether he could be trusted, not after what he'd done to her when she had still been here.

"Do you not feel them?" Invar asked.

Carth shook her head. "I don't detect anything of the shadows. The protections here are too stout for me to be able to do so."

"They have kept from me their plans, Ms. Rel. I cannot tell you where you would find them."

Samis licked his lips and swallowed, as if he were coming to a difficult decision. "They're in the palace," he said. "There's a place beneath the palace…"

Invar looked over to him, head cocked to the side. "They wouldn't use those rooms."

"I'm not sure what's in them, but I heard Evan and some of the others talking about it once. They were excited about what they discovered."

"What is it?" Carth asked, pausing at a staircase inside the palace. She'd spent some time captured within the palace walls, and held in such a way that she couldn't escape, but that hadn't been within the palace itself. She didn't actually think they would have kept her within the palace. Doing so put her too close to others with power.

"A place that has been here since the founding of Nyaesh," Invar said.

"Why does it sound like this is worse than where they kept me?" she asked.

Invar met her gaze. "Because for your kind, it is."

"Samis?" Carth asked. "What do you know?"

He shook his head. "They had a way of removing the Reshian without violating the accords."

"Do you know what that way was?" Carth demanded.

Samis shook his head. "They didn't tell me."

"Then let me. I call them the blood priests. They drain the blood of their victims, and they use it in some twisted magic. They find the Reshian particularly appealing, I think because they can use their blood better and have an immunity to the shadow magic. And now they've drawn the attention of the Hjan." She glared at him. "Tell me, is that worth removing the Reshian? Is it worth it for entire villages to fall? Is that what you would have happen to *me*?"

Samis closed his eyes. "I didn't know."

"Then help us. Let me get the shadow blessed away, and help me stop the blood priests."

Samis looked to Invar before nodding.

Invar went down the flight of stairs before stepping off and leading them down a hall. The walls changed here, less of the solid white stone and more of a grayish rock. Marks on the surface looked almost as if the rock had been dug free by hand. There was no light here, and Invar held his hand out, creating a softly glowing light, enough to push back the darkness. Even here, with all the darkness around her, Carth couldn't detect the shadows.

The suppression might even be more pronounced here.

She strained for them, and could *almost* feel the trailing edge of the shadows, but then it slipped away. The protections within the wall were too potent for her to overcome.

Samis hesitated. "I'll watch the stairs for activity," he said.

She took a slight step toward him. "If you betray us—"

"I made a mistake. I didn't understand."

"You weren't strong enough to question."

Samis breathed out, his shoulders sagging. "I thought I was. I always thought I'd be able to stand up to anything, but when it came down to trusting you or the A'ras, I... I failed, Rel."

She blinked. His admission surprised her, and while she didn't know if she could trust him, she had to try. Wasn't that what she was discovering? She needed the help of others as she tried to understand what they faced.

"Give us warning if something comes."

Samis nodded, his shoulders drawing a little straighter. "You won't have much time."

Carth tapped Dara on the arm and turned down the hall to follow Invar.

The A'ras master hadn't waited for her, and she found him at the end of the hall, stopped at a section of the wall.

He looked over his shoulder and fixed Carth with a steady gaze. "You will need to be ready, Ms. Rel. The other with you as well."

Carth glanced to Dara. "Are you ready?"

"For what?"

Carth shrugged. "I know about as much as you. Just be ready. Do the things we've trained for and you should be fine."

Dara clenched her jaw and nodded once. As she did, power began building from her, a steady burning Carth felt deep beneath her skin. It was a steady sensation, one that started first as a throbbing and then increased to a clearer aching sense.

Carth used her own connection to the S'al and pulled on power, drawing through the ring.

Invar nodded once, as if satisfied now that they had begun pulling on their magic.

He pressed his hand against the wall.

Where he placed it, the stone began to glow. A latticework of pale yellow began crawling out from his hand, creating a trail of writing that Carth couldn't decipher, but that she recognized. It was like the writing in her mother's old books, what she had believed to be Ih-lash writing but now wondered if it might be Lashasn.

Invar tapped a few of the words with his other hand. The glowing seemed to brighten steadily, building with each placement of his hand on additional symbols, so that by the time he rested his other hand on the wall, an entire section of the wall around him glowed with an almost blinding light.

"Evan would have known how to open this?" Carth asked.

Invar shook his head. "Only masters would have known about this," he said softly.

She sensed the disappointment within his voice.

A door slid open.

Light brighter even than the wall poured out.

It slammed against them, a brilliant connection to the S'al, drawing more than she ever had seen, more than even the bright white light she'd suffered through while trapped by Ras. The light was like a weapon that spilled out. Were she not connected to the S'al, she was afraid it might burn through her and destroy her.

"Invar—what is this?"

He didn't look back at her. "This is a place where our ancestors brought those they feared."

"Lashasn ancestors," Carth said.

Invar nodded once.

"And they brought shadow born here, didn't they?" That would be the only reason for such powerful brightness. It would overwhelm anything the shadow born might be able to accomplish, eliminating any possible connection to the shadows.

"At first. The records indicate this was built for someone particularly strong with the shadows. Over time they began using it on others." He took a deep breath and looked back to her. "You must hold on to your connection to the flame, Ms. Rel. If you lose it here, I can't promise what will happen."

"What do you mean?"

"This protection was designed for someone with part of your abilities, though not both of yours. There has never been one so connected to both lines as you, I don't think. But the shadows—you might find that they fade from you while you're here."

"Fade? As in disappear?"

Invar nodded. "This was designed not only to capture, but to eliminate the threat for good."

Carth looked down to her ring and pulled on the power she felt within it, drawing the strength of the S'al as she did. It would have to protect her, but in order for it do so, she would have to be stronger than what she sensed here. Could she?

To save those who had entrusted her with their care, she would. What choice did she have?

Invar stepped across the barrier and into the room.

Carth started forward, but Dara grabbed her arm and held her back.

"Are you certain this is safe for you? If he thinks you need to hold on to your connection to the S'al while in there, what will that do to your other connection?"

"If they're in here, I have to help them."

"What if we help them, and you watch?" Dara asked.

She smiled. Having Dara worry about her was unexpected, and appreciated. "I think I need to do this," she said.

It wasn't only that she needed to help the Reshian they'd brought to Nyaesh; there was a part of her that also needed to know what had been done to the shadow born long ago. She needed to know what the A'ras had once done. It might help her to understand the animosity that remained, and why the accords were such a tenuous peace agreement.

Dara unsheathed her knife and handed it to Carth. "Use this if you need something."

She patted the knife she had sheathed at her waist. "I have one."

"You have one you use with the shadows. This is a knife my father gave me. My mother could use the S'al, but not quite the same way my father could. He was powerful, and had control much like what I see from your Invar." She pointed with the knife. "This was his."

Carth took the knife, feeling the weight of it. Had she remained in the A'ras, she would have forged a knife of her own, adding her strength to it. The only knife she had remaining had been her father's, and that had connected her to the shadows more than to the flame.

"I'll get it back to you."

Dara nodded. "You will."

Carth pulled on the S'al, now using both her ring and the knife. Both augmented her power, allowing her to reach for much more than she could have reached on her own. She drew upon the S'al, taking in as much power as possible.

Then she stepped across the barrier and into the room.

CHAPTER 27

LIGHT SURGED AROUND CARTH.

When she had been trapped by Ras, there had been a bright white light like this, but also a sense of biting cold. That cold had prevented her from reaching the flame, and the brightness to the light had prevented her from reaching the shadows. The combination had held her, confining her inside the cell until Ras had chosen to release it. Carth had never figured it out on her own, thought she had tried.

This light had none of the cold. There was a sense of warmth to it that mixed into the overwhelming brightness, but not warmth like standing under the sun. Her eyes slowly adjusted, taking in the brightness and gradually allowing her to see more than white and yellow.

Invar loomed in front of her, outlined as a lesser glow within the room. She turned and saw Dara coming up behind, dimmer than Invar, but not so much as she would have expected. Dara would be powerful one day, if she was given the chance to train.

Carth wondered what she looked like. Probably not as bright as either of them.

"Where are they?" she asked Invar. Her voice sounded strange. Not muted the way it did when she was wrapped in the shadows. This was almost a sense of emptiness.

Wrapped in this emptiness, she had a sudden surge of fear about what would happen were she to release the connection to the S'al. What would it do to her connection to the shadows? Would it make it fade, the way Invar had warned?

"They will be deeper into this room."

"How deep?" Carth asked.

"Much deeper," Invar said.

He continued onward, and Carth followed him, worried that she might lose him in the enormity of the space. Dara remained close, almost pressing against her back. Carth didn't want to lose her either.

"How does he know how to get through here?" Dara asked softly.

Invar paused and turned to them. "He has gone through here before. He has never expected this place to be used before."

"This is more than a prison," she said as they went further.

"This is more than a prison," Invar agreed.

She felt power around her but didn't know why that should be. Why would she be aware of the power, almost as if someone used the A'ras magic here?

A terrifying thought came to her. Could all of this be powered, much like the flame in the Master Hall?

Carth decided to test it.

She pressed out, using a hint of power, enough that she could push out against the brightness she detected around her.

If it was like the flame in the Master Hall, it would dim.

It did, but only slightly.

"Careful, Ms. Rel. This is an ancient construct and one that even the masters here did not fully understand. We would not have been able to recreate it."

Carth stopped pushing against the light but held tightly to the power coursing through her.

Invar stopped.

Carth looked, searching for sign that there might be others here, but didn't see anything. The light was too bright around her, too overwhelming. She noted shades of brightness, but that was all that she could see.

"Invar?"

"They will be here, Ms. Rel," he said. His voice was soft and echoed strangely.

Carth didn't see any shift to the intensity of light, nothing that would indicate there was someone else here with them, but then would she? Invar used the A'ras flame in order for her to see him, as did Dara. Those of Reshian wouldn't be able to do so.

Worse, the shadow connection they did possess would be stifled.

"How will we know? Are they chained somewhere?"

He shook his head. "There is no need for chains, Ms.

Rel. This type of enclosure is such that it would be unnecessary. Imagine what you would experience without your connection to the flame."

That meant this was exactly like what Ras had used against her, only with a twist so that it would counter both of her abilities. How would he have known how to do this?

Ras had managed to navigate in the brightness and find her, but then, he had placed her in such a way that there were only a few places she could have gone. Was this the same? Would it direct her the way that Ras had directed her?

"Can you find them?"

"Eventually."

"We might not have time, not if the others of the A'ras reach us first."

"I am aware of our time constraints," Invar said. "It takes time to navigate and find where they would go. This is designed to confine them, not us."

Carth knew how she would find where they might have been held, but it required her to do something she didn't know whether it was safe for her to do. Would her connection to the shadows fade? Would she lose it completely and not be able to regain it?

To find the others, those she had put in danger by bringing them to Nyaesh, she had no other choice.

She released her connection to the S'al.

Pain surged through her and she staggered.

"Follow me," she said.

"Carth?" Dara cried.

"Follow. Me." The pain pushed on her. She had felt

something like this before, but it was even worse than what she had experienced when she was under Ras's control. This was like fire racing through her blood, as if everything she knew had been burned away. She could feel the part of the shadows that she knew, the part that she should be able to detect, fading. There was no other word for it, nothing other than fading. There was nothing.

Carth staggered again, the pressure from the light and the warmth pushing on her. It overwhelmed her, but she knew what she needed to do. She needed to find her way toward where the light pushed her. She needed to find the children of Ih.

She was distantly aware of the presence of Dara's hand on her back, clutching at her cloak. Did she even still hold on to the knife? Squeezing her hand, she felt the hilt of it press into her palm.

The light pushed her and she followed.

The pain eased as she did, growing gradually less, though not lessening completely. In that way, it was just like what she had experienced with Ras.

"You need to reach the S'al," Dara whispered.

"The S'al blocks me from reaching what I need," she said.

The pressure of the light pushed.

She could do nothing more than follow. What other choice did she have?

Then it eased.

Nearby, she heard whimpering.

"Andin? Lindy?" She cried out their names.

"C-Carth?"

She reached for the nearest voice. Hand gripped hers and squeezed. "I'm here," she said.

"They caught you too?"

This was Lindy. She knelt, and Carth imagined her face pressing up against her though she couldn't see it. "I'm here to help."

"There is no help," Andin's voice called through the brightness.

"Take my hands," she said. "I'll see you out."

"How? You're trapped the same as the rest of us. There's nothing, Carth!"

"Andin!" Lindy snapped.

"It's her fault that we're here," Andin said. "We trusted her and she led us here. She claimed a truce, that peace would keep us safe, but there is no peace, not for us. We're from Isahl, and they are descendants of Lashasn."

"We might be descended from Lashasn, but that doesn't mean we all agree with your treatment," Invar said.

He practically glowed, and Dara next to him as well.

Now that she was here, and now that she was with them, she pressed through her mother's ring, through the knife that Dara had lent her, and reached for the power of the S'al.

It flowed slowly at first, as if even that ability had faded.

Carth pulled on it, raging against the connection. When it came, it did so suddenly, and with a fury.

"Carth?" Dara asked.

She surged again, drawing more and more of the power in this room.

The walls flickered.

It was subtle, but she *saw* it this time.

With it came a surprising faint connection to the shadows.

They were there, but distant and muted, like a soft edge of shadows on a bright summer day. Carth pressed again, this time pulsing outward with all the strength she could summon through both the knife and the ring. This time, there was a definite connection to the shadows.

"Ms. Rel, what you are doing is dangerous. We must depart if you are to get them to safety."

"If they can reach the shadows, they will be safe," she said.

"You risk exposing our presence here before we have a chance to understand all that has taken place."

Carth noted brighter shapes in the distance. She had *felt* them as well, especially while pulsing with the S'al. "I think our presence has already been exposed."

She tapped on Dara's hand. "We need to reach the doorway. Can you find it?"

"I… I think so."

"Invar. You can't be caught here with us."

"Ms. Rel, I think I can take care of myself."

"I need someone trustworthy in the A'ras," she said. "Someone who recognizes the value of the accords. If you're caught with me, there won't be anyone here who will be able to help. Please, Invar. Mask yourself."

He stepped close to her. She felt him as much as she saw him. When he grabbed her arm, she felt strength in the grip. "Move carefully, Ms. Rel. If you press too hard against the flame, even you can get burned."

She smiled but knew he couldn't see it. "Don't forget, Invar, that I can use both shadows and flame." Turning to the others, she said, "Come on. Hold on to each other and we'll get free."

Dara slipped past and started away, though not in the direction Carth would have expected they needed to go. She had to trust Dara, so she trailed after her, this time holding on to her.

They grabbed onto her cloak and followed, trailing her. She couldn't see them the same way she saw Dara… or the way she saw the three A'ras coming toward them.

"We have to hurry, Dara."

"I see them."

They weren't going to move fast enough. The Reshian could follow closely, but they were limited in that they couldn't see anything but the brightness of the light. Carth doubted that they would even be able to make them out. Were it not for the physical connection, they might not be able to stay with them.

Carth took the hand of the person who held on to her and placed it on Dara's back. "Go!" she urged. "Get out of the room and I'll join you."

"Carth?" Dara asked.

"Just go."

They slipped around her.

Carth turned toward the approaching A'ras. They moved more quickly than the Reshian were able to move, and Carth would have to intervene.

She unsheathed her father's knife and held it in her opposite hand. Armed now with knives for shadow and light, she strained for her connection to the flame and pressed outward.

Power surged, and the light within the room dimmed.

It was subtle, slight, but she felt the edge of the shadows and grasped for it.

And missed.

Carth pulsed again, this time with more force than before. There came an echoing pulse, and she recognized Invar helping her.

The light within the room dimmed slightly more.

She grasped for the shadows. They were there—faint, but there.

Then she reached them.

And the A'ras reached her.

These were A'ras, but if they were responsible for attacking the children of Isahl, and if they were responsible for coordinating the attacks with the blood priests, they were no longer her allies.

Carth struck, not only with the flame of the A'ras but with the shadows, ducking as she went, cutting at them until she caught the nearest person with the knife and pressed shadows into the blade. When she'd attacked near Master Hall, she had wanted to incapacitate rather than harm. This time, she had seen others tormented and she would do what it took to see them to safety, even if it meant attacking when she didn't want to.

The person fell.

The other A'ras turned toward her.

She pressed outward with the A'ras connection again and pulled on the shadows once more, sending these out through the knife as she attacked. The combination of shadow and flame was too much for the A'ras, but she had other ways of attacking and wasn't reliant on only that.

Swinging her leg around, she kicked.

The combination of her abilities gave her an advantage —she could tell where the A'ras were, and they might not be able to see her.

A blade whistled toward her and she caught it with her knife, deflecting it.

Carth rolled, kicking out toward the brightness she saw.

There was a satisfying grunt.

She kicked toward the A'ras and caught the person another time, and then another. The attack stopped.

Where was the third?

She didn't see them.

Carth looked around, but they weren't nearby.

That meant they'd gone after the others.

Carth searched for Dara and saw her as a faint glow.

She raced toward her. As she did, another form appeared, near enough to Dara that Carth worried for her friend.

Nearing, she launched herself, not willing to wait any longer.

Her attack caught the other in the midsection. She heard a soft grunt and flipped around, kicking as she did. The kick missed, but the next one didn't, connecting somewhere near the head. The A'ras attacker crumpled.

She slipped toward Dara.

"Carth?" Dara asked.

"It's me."

"How are you able to attack?"

Carth didn't get the chance to answer.

Something struck her from behind, sending her staggering forward.

Carth braced herself as she landed. One of the knives clattered from her hand—the Lashasn knife she'd borrowed from Dara. She scrambled for it when pain bit into her leg.

Fire shot through her.

But it was a fire she recognized.

This was the pain of A'ras that burned in her.

Carth reached for the connection. She drew through the ring, using the pain burning through her blood, and even drawing through the person who attacked her, somehow using whatever ability he possessed to press outward, and sent a blasting surge of power away from her.

The A'ras screamed.

Carth grabbed for the shadows at the same time. There was more of an edge, as if what she'd done had created more of a shadow. Using this, she sliced, cutting into the A'ras attacker.

The knife bit into flesh and she sent the shadows out into him, releasing them from her. She'd seen the way the shadows would crawl free, the way they would damage a person when they were unleashed. She didn't want to kill —not the way she'd been willing to do when Felyn had attacked her and she'd used the shadows—but she needed to use the shadows to slow her attacker.

There was another scream.

She crawled forward, her hand closing on the knife she'd dropped.

Someone grabbed her by the arm and pulled her forward. Carth fought, struggling against it, until she was thrown forward. As she did, she passed through the barrier and was once more in the hall.

Carth looked up and saw Samis following her through the door.

Had the others gotten free? Had they succeeded?

Huddled near the wall, she saw the six from Reshian. Lindy watched her with wide eyes. Dara stood near them, but a step away, as if she didn't want to get too close to them.

"Rel, you have to go," Samis said.

She looked up at him.

"I'll do what I can to buy you some time, but you need to leave."

"Not yet."

"What?"

"If they're responsible for calling the blood priests, I will draw them out."

"You can't do that, Rel."

"If I want a real peace, I don't have a choice."

She staggered forward, the pain in her leg returning, and grabbed Dara as she motioned to the Reshian to follow before heading up the stairs.

CHAPTER 28

CARTH STARTED INTO THE HALL AND BACK UP THE STAIRS. They didn't see anyone, and Carth felt nervous. Why weren't there more of the A'ras here?

The answer came when they reached outside the palace. A dozen A'ras were arranged outside, waiting for her. She recognized half of them and had been friendly with Erin, the woman who stood in the center with her sword unsheathed. Did Erin now lead the A'ras?

Had she betrayed the accords?

She had blamed the Hjan, but maybe it wasn't the Hjan at all. Could the *A'ras* be the reason the accords failed? They should *want* the accords. It prevented fighting with the Reshian, and allowed them to have peace. Why abandon that?

A'ras power flowed around her, practically crackling in the air.

Carth touched the hilt of her knife. She hadn't wanted to believe the A'ras would intentionally attempt to violate the accords, but what other answer was there? Wasn't that the reason Samis had tried keeping her away?

"You don't have to attack," she said. "You never had to attack. The Reshian were not a threat."

"The Reshian attacked Nyaesh," Erin said.

"They didn't. They attacked the Hjan, but even if they did, the A'ras agreed to the accords the same as the Reshian."

"The accords. That has done nothing to stop the Reshian from attacking," Erin said. "The masters chose to do nothing, but we will see the threat ended."

"By destroying people who agreed to peace?" She took a step toward Erin.

"We have done nothing."

"No. You let the blood priests destroy the Reshian."

"We have not violated the accords," Erin said. "The Reshian have."

"Because the remaining Reshian blame Lashasn."

"They were never trustworthy."

"They were never given a chance." That bothered her more than anything. "I will see that the fighting stops."

Erin laughed. "No one will believe you. You ran from the city, nothing more than a Reshian spy."

Carth sighed. The longer they stayed here, the more they risked others coming from behind and attacking. "I was no spy. I use the same flame as you." To prove it, she pulled on the A'ras magic, drawing from the flame, letting it fill her. "Would a Reshian spy be able to use the A'ras magic?"

"Yes."

She wasn't going to convince her, and maybe she

didn't need to. All she needed to care about right now was getting the Reshian out of the city and back on the ship. Then she could find a way to stop the next attack. And the next.

But was that even the answer? They needed peace. Real peace.

To do so would require fighting. Strange that it often did.

"You have betrayed the A'ras coordinating with the blood priests," Carth said.

"We have coordinated with nothing—"

"The rest of the A'ras will know, even if they do not now." Others of the A'ras had appeared. They stood behind Erin, watching. Could she convince them? Somehow, she would have to, especially if she were to get their help. "Not all of you seek violence."

Erin narrowed her eyes. "What do you think you can do?"

"I won't have to do anything. The A'ras will find the appropriate justice." She turned, preparing to fight. "Those of you who want peace, know that there are some among you who want otherwise. They have partnered with a violent magic to attack the Reshian, which only made them think the A'ras attacked."

That perception would make it so the Reshian would believe the A'ras attacked, and the A'ras could claim innocence while defending themselves. It was a dangerous game, and one that left her with only a few moves.

"I have uncovered the truth. I am the reason the accords were established. I will not allow them to fall."

She had not wanted the recognition, but if it would

bring a lasting peace, she would force them to acknowledge her role in establishing peace.

All around her, the A'ras watched. Listening.

Some would be convinced. Not all wanted to fight.

The A'ras nearest her approached. They were skilled—she could detect that in the way they used the power of the flame—and if she weren't careful, some of the children of Isahl would suffer.

That was unacceptable.

The alternative was fighting, but that forced her away from the move she wanted to make.

Was there an alternative?

She felt a pulsing of flame. Invar.

Would he act?

He had remained reluctant, but now that he knew what had happened, how the others had intended for an attack, how could he not act?

"Dara," Carth started, motioning toward her friend, "you need to focus your attention on the wall we came through. Do you remember it?"

"The wall?"

Carth drew on the strength of the S'al, letting it fill her in ways that it never had when she'd lived here. As it did, she unleashed it.

Dara followed suit.

The magic streaked away. When it hit the wall, it exploded.

Shadows leached in.

Andin gasped.

"Don't hurt them," she said softly, using the shadows to shield her voice. "We need only to escape."

The others of Reshian sank into the shadows, practically disappearing. Only Andin strode forward. He surged out with his attack, a powerful strike of the shadow born. Three of the nearest A'ras fell before his shadows, caught in a writhing tangle of them.

"Andin!" she shouted.

He strode forward and sent another attack. Three more of the A'ras fell.

He continued to hold on to the connection to the shadows, but this time when he unleashed, the remaining A'ras were ready.

Flames met his attack.

Erin darted forward, sword unsheathed.

Carth lunged, catching the sword with only her knife and pushing it back. "Dara! Take them to the ship!"

She couldn't tell if her friend listened.

Hating that she had to attack, Carth ran toward the Andin. Using mostly her shadows, she suppressed his attack, preventing him from striking the A'ras again. If he continued to fight, they would lose the tenuous peace they'd managed to hold.

Andin fell back from her.

She needed to incapacitate him so that he didn't continue to fight. She didn't want to hurt him, but then, she didn't want to get stuck in the middle of the A'ras and him fighting either.

How would Ras attack?

She thought about what he had done, and the way that he'd shed her attack when she'd used the shadows. Was there anything in that she could learn and take from?

He had used his connection to the Lashasn magic.

Carth collected it, drawing it through the ring, and breathed it out.

Light surged.

It flowed over Andin.

She felt him attempt to press through the shimmering power she'd released, but he failed.

Carth pulled on her Lashasn connection again, this time she breathed it out with even more force. The power flowed out from her and struck him again, clinging to him.

A'ras power built behind her.

She spun and drew the shadows around her, collecting them in such a way that she shielded both her and Andin. It did nothing to attack the A'ras, but it should buy them time.

Grabbing Andin, she pulled him along with her and made her way toward the destroyed wall. "What were you thinking?" she demanded.

"Me? They took us off the ship and brought us to that… that place. There was nothingness there. I couldn't reach the shadows. It was like they had been burned off of me."

"That was a mistake," Carth said. "Don't make another by fighting when another solution would work better."

They reached the wall. Carth took in the effect of both her and Dara's attack. The wall had caved here, leaving a huge gaping hole in the wall. Behind her, she heard the sound of fighting, but didn't dare wait to see if Invar had managed to gain control of the A'ras as she hoped. Waiting any longer would prevent them from reaching the ship. And she had to know what was going on.

"Go!" she said. "Get back on the ship."

"Where are you going?"

"I'm going to keep you from doing anything stupid."

She waited for him to take off, and when he had, she turned back toward the A'ras. Standing near the remnants of the wall, she drew the shadows around her, pulling from where the wall overlooked the rest of the yard. Standing here allowed her to ignore the separation the wall created, and the magic infused into the wall, and let her reach beyond the A'ras connection that segregated the shadows.

Then she pushed them away from her.

They rolled, something like a fog.

A'ras magic surged, and Carth could feel the individual efforts drawing on it and pushed the shadows against them, suppressing their ability. If any of them managed to reach the A'ras flame, they would be able to push against the shadows.

It held.

She didn't want to harm them. She might need them, especially if her plan should work. And she needed them to know the Reshian—those who could use the shadows—would not harm them.

She pushed outward, slowing them.

Flame exploded. Power came from near the tower.

Others of the A'ras came.

There were dozens of them, power building, leaving Carth's skin burning.

Invar led them, meeting her gaze as he approached. Power exploded from him, almost as much as she could summon.

The others of the A'ras turned to him.

She needed Invar. Without him, the next part of her plan would not work.

His voice boomed, clearing the heat. "Enough!" he roared. He was an A'ras Master, finally claiming his position.

Carth smiled to herself.

This was not a fight she needed to participate in. Invar would see the A'ras fell back into line. It surprised her that it took so long for him to do so.

Holding tightly to the shadows, she stepped through the wall and raced through the streets.

When she reached River Road, she hurried to the ship. The others had just gotten aboard, and she jumped from the dock onto the ship, using the shadows to power her as she did.

"Time to go, Guya," she said, "but only into the river."

He looked over to her as if unsurprised that she would appear on the deck of the ship without any other warning. "I've got her untied, now just need to get her underway."

Carth focused on the water, and the darkness beneath the docks. Using this, she pulled on these shadows, rippling them against the hull and sliding the ship out into the water.

Andin reached her and seemed to realize what she was doing. He added his own touch to it, and together, they pushed the ship out from the dock and into the sea.

Carth held on to the shadows, protecting the ship now, no longer attempting to push it out into the water, but not bothering to hide her abilities. Rather, she wanted to demonstrate them. That was the next part of her plan.

Andin watched her, his jaw clenched.

Carth began to detect the distinct sense of pressure against her shadow ability. She glanced to Andin, noting the way his eyes went wide, and knew that he detected it as well. It was too soon, but then, if the A'ras had been working with the blood priests, they would have alerted them, wouldn't they?

"You've sensed this before?" she asked. The last time she'd felt this pressure had been with the blood priests, but they hadn't gotten close enough for Andin to detect them.

"This is Lashasn."

"Not Lashasn. This is the blood priests."

His eyes widened. "I know what you've said about them. They'll kill us. Take our blood for their power. And you want to bring them here?"

Carth closed her eyes as she stepped to the railing. She let her sense of the shadows drift away from her and took his hand and had him stand with her at the railing. "For you to remain safe—and for peace to hold—I will need your help."

"Let's sail from here. Let the A'ras deal with them."

Carth knew they wouldn't come after the A'ras. They would chase the shadow blessed. They would continue to do so until they captured them and stole the magic they possessed. And then they would use this in their horrible ceremony. She was determined to stop them for good. She was determined to see peace hold.

"We need to draw them here."

Andin stared at her, his eyes like saucers. "Why? Why

would you try to bring them in? You know what they want and why they want us."

Carth leaned on the edge of the ship. "Drawing them in is only the next move."

"And you need me?"

"I need shadow strength. They have to know we're here."

"And when they do?"

"Then you'll have to trust me."

Andin frowned, but slowly he nodded. That was good. Carth would need him to agree to what she planned. Invar and the A'ras would have to help, but this required shadow power. She needed Andin to help demonstrate it, to draw the blood priests.

"How can you protect us if they come?" Andin asked.

"That's the hard part," Carth said.

"Why?"

"You'll have to return to the prison of light buried beneath the palace."

CHAPTER 29

CARTH STOOD AT THE HELM OF THE SHIP, GRIPPING THE wheel, feeling like an imposter as she took control of Guya's vessel. She was not alone on the *Goth Spald*; Alison, Samis, and Invar traveled with her. Dara remained with the shadow blessed. She could protect them in a way that took a certain sacrifice from them, and she had agreed to work with Lindy and Andin to do so. If they were attacked by the blood priests, Lindy and Andin's abilities would be negated, but Dara's would not. She offered them some protection. The A'ras would provide the remaining protection.

Alison stood next to Carth, her slight frame belying the strength Carth knew existed within her. She was her oldest friend, but that friendship had changed. She no longer knew what to make of their connection, if one remained, just as she no longer knew what to make of the friendship she had once had with Samis. He stood on the raised section near the stern, staring out over the sea, his eyes flickering, as if uncertain.

Carth understood his uncertainty; she had taken him away from what he knew, even if only briefly. She had taken him away from the A'ras and brought them into a fight that he had nothing to do with. If this went well, he could return and she wouldn't ask anything more of him.

If it went well.

Invar remained statuesque, standing with his hands tucked in the sleeves of his cloak. He looked regal in some ways. He was one of the few within the A'ras who could reach the true power of the flame, descended from Lashasn, much like Carth and Dara. There were secrets to him, she suspected, but he had not seen fit to answer them.

"Do you think we can catch these… what do you call them?... blood priests?" Alison asked.

Carth hung on to the shadows, pushing out from her. Bait. They were on a ship, so it made sense that they would go fishing. She wanted to draw the blood priests to her.

With the rest of the shadow blessed safe within the strange prison buried beneath the palace of Nyaesh, the blood priests wouldn't be able to detect the use of the shadows. Lindy and Andin had gone reluctantly when Carth had explained her plan. Dara had seen what she intended. She had been willing to stand with them, to use her connection to the S'al to press back the oppression caused by the light prison, and keep the remaining youth of Ih-lash safe.

"I don't intend to catch them. I intend to bring them to

me." She stared into the growing night. It was fitting for her to attack now, and they would be more likely to draw the blood priests to them. "Let them attack. Let them see what the A'ras can do."

Alison shook her head and nodded towards Invar. "You're using the A'ras, the same way you didn't want to be used yourself."

Carth fixed Alison with a hard-eyed gaze. Had she not once been betrayed by the A'ras, she might feel differently about using them. But now they were a piece on a game board, no different than they had been when she used them to negotiate for peace. This time, she didn't think there could be peace. She didn't intend for there to be any treaties signed, as she didn't think the blood priests would abide by such treaties. She intended to eradicate their threat. That was the only way to keep the remaining shadow blessed safe.

"They attacked because of the A'ras. If the A'ras work with Isahl, then we can prove that peace should still hold."

"That is all?"

"They are as much a threat to the A'ras as they are to the Reshian."

Carth left Alison and made her way towards Invar. He had come to assist, but he had come reluctantly. He was tied to the city in ways that Carth was not, but he was also tied to the descendants of Lashasn in the same ways she was. "You haven't said much."

Invar turned his attention to her. He had a heavy gaze, one that had once intimidated her, but now there was a quiet introspection about the man. He had shown himself willing to help her even when it might cost him. Then again, that had come at a time when the other masters had thought him growing incompetent. They had thought to depose him and had been willing to work with the Hjan even knowing they had attacked the A'ras.

He sighed. "I worry what it means that we seek to destroy rather than create."

Carth thought of the destruction she had seen. Those villages empty along the coast, villages she now knew had been destroyed, the bodies bled out and drained in the brutal ceremony the blood priest used to build their magic. Entire ships painted with the blood of their victims. There could be no peace.

"I pray that you never fully understand."

Invar considered her with a gaze that carried a certain sadness to it. "You have changed, Ms. Rel. You were so tentative and yet bold at the same time. Now you are calculating. I suspect that is the effect of your time with Ras?"

Calculating. She wanted to be calculating, but there were times when she didn't think she thought nearly as far ahead as she needed to. She'd been surprised by these blood priests, taken aback by the power of their blood magic, taken aback by the brutality—something that was different even than what she had seen with the Hjan. How could such brutality exist?

It should not. It would not.

As she held on to the shadows, clutching them furiously, expending all her strength to hold on to them, she felt pressure build around her. This was a familiar sense. She recognized it as an attack, coming from the blood priests.

She nodded to Invar. "They come."

"I'm not certain our preparations will be enough."

Carth let out a deep breath. "They will have to be. Had you managed to maintain control…"

"I was trying to hold the A'ras together."

"By letting them tear apart peace?"

Invar sighed. "There was only so much I could do. I had hoped getting word to the C'than would have allowed them to take action."

The C'than. At least now she understood Ras's move. He had *wanted* her to go to Isahl and then come to Nyaesh.

"Damn you, Ras," she whispered.

Invar watched her as she moved to the bow so that she could focus on the sense of the blood priests pressing on her shadows. She needed to detect what they did, needed to know where they were. She had placed other lives in danger to protect the lives of the shadow blessed.

Carth nodded to Invar. "You have some way of communicating to the others along the shore?"

Invar nodded.

Carth clenched her jaw. Would he keep from her how he did this?

"Make sure they are ready," Carth said.

Invar closed his eyes and Carth detected a whisper of the flame from him, something with a specific signature. She followed it, noting how it trailed back towards the shore, touching several distinct places as it did.

This was the connection.

Carth smiled to herself with relief. Invar hadn't kept

his ability from her, but he expected her to recognize what he did.

Power built against the shadows, slowly collapsing upon her. This was nothing like what she had experienced upon the sea twice before.

How many of the blood priests came?

She feared what they would be able to do when they did come. Most of all, she feared what would happen to those of the A'ras if they were unprepared.

But… she didn't *need* to fear. The A'ras were dangerous. They were swordsmen. They were practitioners of magic. They could craft the flame. All those abilities made them a deadly foe for the blood priests. It was why they had never ventured up the river, why they had never ventured towards Nyaesh.

Carth began to withdraw the shadows. The first ship came into view.

The hull was painted a deep red with sails to match. She pointed. "That's their blood magic," she said softly.

His eyes tightened as he frowned deeply, studying the ship. He pressed out with a gentle probe using the flame. Carth hadn't realized how attuned she had become to the flame, having only practiced with Dara and not with any others powered the same as her. She followed how Invar traced his connection along the hull, trailing it up towards the sails. Then he withdrew. "The A'ras used them?"

Carth nodded.

"So reckless."

"That is the blood of their victims. That is the blood of countless villagers dead along the shores."

Invar closed his eyes once more and sent another

pulse of flame, stretching it away from him. When it retreated once more, his eyes snapped open, an ashen expression coming across his face. "There are others still trapped on that ship."

Carth had feared that. "They kept others alive the first time we met them as well."

"You intend to save them." It was a statement rather than a question.

Carth nodded. That was the biggest reason she needed the help of the A'ras. She could fight the blood priests; she thought she could destroy their ships. But could she do so and rescue those still trapped within? That was what she needed to do.

Invar turned his attention back to Alison and Samis. "I will convince them. They will fight with you." He rested his hand on her arm. Her skin tingled where he touched her. "Ms. Rel, this is the right thing to do."

Carth knew that it was, but Invar's reassurance uplifted her somewhat.

"How do you intend to attack?"

"They came for the descendants of Ih. I think it's time they fear the descendants of Lashasn."

CHAPTER 30

CARTH SWAM TOWARDS THE BLOOD PRIESTS' SHIP. THE current was heavy but heading in this direction, so she swam with it as opposed to against it. She didn't fear the water, not as so many did. When she reached the hull of the ship, she placed her hand just above the surface. There was a strange pulsing power that emanated from the ship. The blood priest magic.

Taking a deep breath, she pressed power through her hand, through the ring, and into the hull of the ship.

The magic resisted, but she used the power of the flame as opposed to the shadows. This was more powerful than what the blood priests were capable of withstanding. A small hole gradually appeared. She burned it with increasing force, creating an opening. When it was wide enough, Carth crawled inside.

She held her hand open and used the power of the flame to keep her ring lit, letting it glow and create enough light to see. She didn't dare use the shadows, fearing that they would draw the attention of the blood priests. It was possible they knew she was here already, and if they did, her plan to save those on the ship would fail, and she'd be forced to destroy them. That was her final plan.

Once inside, she crawled forward. She didn't have to search long to find the captives. The power of the flame magic practically showed her where to find them. Well over a dozen remained within the hull of the ship, but how many more had been lost?

She reached a closed door and burned her way through. The faces inside cowered away from her.

Carth raised a finger to her lips and motioned for them to follow. "Come with me and I will get you free."

She pointed in the direction of the opening in the hull. The women—they were all women, she noted—followed her. Most had dirty faces and frightened eyes that looked as if they didn't dare to hope. She couldn't imagine the horrors they must've experienced.

Carth helped them to the edge of the ship. "Swim. There are others who will help you from here."

The first woman hesitated, but Carth nodded, trying to reassure her. She climbed down from the ship and into the water with barely a splash. Others followed, one after another.

When the ship was empty, Carth returned to the holding area and placed an A'ras knife into the center of the room. She backed away and reached the door when she felt a dark presence against her.

Carth spun and saw a blood priest watching her.

He had wide eyes and pale skin, much like the rest of

them she had seen. Maroon stained his cheeks and his neck, a dark color so deep it appeared permanent.

How many times had he painted his face? She didn't let herself think about what he would have done to take on such darkness.

He didn't speak as he attacked.

Carth didn't give him a chance to reach her. She jumped back, sliding on the shadows, now wanting to draw the attention of the blood priest. When she reached the opening she'd created, she jumped into the water. She shifted her focus from the shadows to the flame, pressing through the knife she'd left within the holding area, using it as a focus.

She wanted nothing more than violence and explosion.

Heat built rapidly from her, coming from deep within her. It burned through her skin, and burned through her blood.

The ship exploded.

Carth swam, reaching one of the other women. She helped them until they reached the *Goth Spald*, where the A'ras helped them on board.

Invar watched her. "What now, Ms. Rel?" he asked.

There were seven ships left, but would they be strong enough to stop them? Would they be able to slow the blood priests?

What choice did they have?

"One down."

Fire erupted in the sky.

The blood priests seemed to recognize they were under attack. Their ships attempted to turn, but Lashasn power held on to them. Carth had rescued two more shiploads of women. Only women. It troubled her that the men were gone. Why would they have the women? How many were Reshian?

Those would be questions for later.

The two she had attacked after the first had been smaller ships. Their holds only carried five or six people, but they were painted the same blood red as the others. Invar had led the attack on others, his explosions much more controlled than hers.

Carth now detected two ships remaining, and they pressed upon her shadow awareness more strongly than the others. She feared what she would find when she reached them. How many of the blood priests would be on board a ship like that?

The timing was important now.

If she waited too long, the ships would turn and escape. Already she could feel them trying to pull away from the Lashasn attack.

Invar led the attack on one while she went for the other, this one much larger than any of the others. When she reached the ship, she realized they were nearly side by side. Invar had already created a hole in the hull of the ship. Carth acted quickly, using the power of her S'al magic to burn through the ship. When she climbed inside, the bitter stink of the blood priests attacked her first.

A horrific scene met her eyes. Blood was spattered all over the inside of the ship. Bodies were strewn about, most looking as if they had been trying to crawl away as they were attacked. A dozen blood priests stood before her, all with fresh, sticky blood coating their bodies.

Anger rose within her.

How could they do something like this? How could they use people in such a casual way?

She no longer suppressed the shadows, pressing them out from her.

As she did, there was something of an answer, pulsing against her.

Had Andin made a mistake and left the holding room?

It would be dangerous if true.

And it would mean she had to act faster.

None of the blood priests spoke as they arranged themselves around her. Power rippled beneath their skin, but they didn't transform as the others she had seen had done.

Carth pulled the only weapon she had remaining. It was her shadow knife, the one she had found near her mother after she had been killed. This was the knife that helped with controlling the shadows. This was the knife she suspected was her father's but had never confirmed it. It would not help her hone her connection to the flame, but it was all she had.

One of the blood priests smiled, as if detecting her hesitation.

Carth played out the different options in her mind.

There were only a few moves that might succeed here. Her intent had been to rescue the girls from the ship, but that was no longer possible. Now... now her goal was to destroy the blood priests so they could harm no one else and prevent the violence the cabal within the A'ras intended for the Reshian. As she played this out, she realized there might be no other option for her other than to sacrifice herself.

Doing so would stop the blood priests.

Invar had seen what she was willing to do to maintain the accords. Hopefully Andin and the others of Isahl would understand as well. If they didn't, peace *would* fall. Everything she'd fought for would fail.

All she wanted was peace.

What move could she make?

The game played out in her mind. This was the only option.

She slammed the knife into the ship. She would use the focus of the S'al magic and press it through her mother's ring, use that to grant her increased strength. She might not have a knife that could help focus her magic, but she had her mother's ring.

The blood priests closed on her. She felt them converging, felt the way they pressed against her connection to the shadows.

Carth began building power.

The priest reached for her.

Carth pulsed all the Lashasn magic into the ring and through the knife. Unwittingly, she added that of the shadows as well.

They fused, creating a combination of power, of the magic she possessed, creating something *more*.

Something similar had happened in the past, and just as before, she had no control over it. Power burned with dark intensity. Carth pressed out through the knife, through the ring, and it exploded from her.

She sank to her knees. Wetness caught her legs and it took a moment to realize that she was in the water.

She opened her eyes. A ship came toward her. It wasn't a blood priest ship—or the A'ras.

Reshian.

Carth looked up to see the captain watching her. There were others on the deck, and all were armed with a strange sort of flaming arrows.

"Father?"

A rope dropped toward her and she reached for it, looking around as she did.

The moon hung overhead, bright and staring at her as if smiling. She turned, but nothing of the ship she'd destroyed remained. Nearby, the other ship, the one Invar had attacked, slowly sank as well. A raft carrying nearly three dozen people drifted away.

Carth finally allowed herself to smile.

CHAPTER 31

"The peace will hold."

Carth considered her father. "That's all you have to say to me?"

"That is what you wanted, isn't it?"

She stood on the deck of his ship, exhausted. Invar was nearby but said nothing. The A'ras had found—and ended —the blood priests.

The remnants of Isahl had been brought aboard and were getting examined for any injuries, but there were none. Andin watched her, his dark eyes suspicious even of the Reshian. Would that ever fade? Lindy said nothing, but she remained close to Carth, as if she didn't intend to leave her alone.

"That is what I wanted."

"We will work together to remove the remaining threat," her father said.

She glanced over to Invar. He nodded. That would have been a difficult concession for the A'ras to agree to help the Reshian, but it was a good one. There weren't many of the Reshian remaining. The women she'd rescued from the ships hadn't been Reshian, and from what she had gathered, they had lost nearly all of their people. Only a few ships remained. Would they be able to rebuild with that?

"How are you here?" The question hadn't come to her quickly enough, but it came now.

"How? We've hidden here."

Carth looked at the Reshian ships. There were so few remaining. "Here?" Her mind lurched through what she knew, and she shook her head. "You remained concealed, didn't you?"

Her father held her with a hard gaze. "We were not going to let them slaughter us. They use the blood of the Reshian—"

"I know."

He sighed, looking at the A'ras on his ship as well as those arranged on the shore. "They helped. They stopped the fighting."

"I didn't leave them much of a choice."

He smiled and it was the kind of smile she remembered from when she was younger. "Good."

"Not good. Peace needs to hold. The Hjan *want* the accords to fail."

"I said that it will."

She looked to Invar. "You have to uphold your end. The A'ras must find a way to maintain the peace as well," she said.

"We will, Ms. Rel."

She nodded and started toward the railing.

"Carthenne—"

She shook her head. She'd spent months wondering what she would say to her father if she could reach him, and now that he was here with her, she didn't know what she wanted. A chance to relax. Perhaps that was all that she wanted.

"You are C'than?" she asked.

He met her eyes and then shook his head. "I am not."

She frowned. She'd thought that was what Ras had meant by suggesting she find her father, and the reason that her father had come here. Was there a different reason?

"You know of them."

"I know that they work in the shadows, manipulating events," he said.

"Interesting choice of words for a shadow born."

"It was intentional. The C'than are even more secretive than the Hjan." He reached a hand out, as if to pat her on the shoulder, and she stiffened. It would be a while before she could find that warmth welcome. "You did well bringing the shadow blessed with you. They can study with those of us who remain. As could you."

Carth sighed. That had been what she'd wanted, but now she didn't think it was.

"Peace will hold," Carth said.

"Yes."

"Good. Then I don't need to remain any longer." She'd been uncertain about what she would do, but if peace *would* hold, then she wasn't needed.

"You could help ensure that it does," her father said. "I could work with you—"

"You could have worked with me years ago." There wasn't the hurt in the words like there had been before. Now it was only a statement of fact.

"I could have, but you wouldn't have developed into who you are today." He patted her arm, and this time she didn't tense. "What will you do now?"

Carth glanced over to Guya, standing on the *Goth Spald*. She hadn't known, not before now, but the answer was obvious. If peace would hold in the north, then she needed to get back to what she'd intended after forging the accords.

"I will go south."

"Why south? The Hjan?"

She nodded. "It's time I learn more. There's one among them who claimed I know nothing. I intend to change that." And she needed to know if the Hjan *had* infiltrated the C'than. She didn't know what to make of them other than that they were powerful—and likely had used her.

She smiled to herself. If Ras *had* played her, she could be nothing but impressed. Perhaps now it was time for her to find a way to use them as well.

They might not want to face the Hjan, but she would see that they had no choice.

"You are always welcome among the Reshian, Carthenne."

"You might not want me. If peace fails, I will learn and I will return."

"I would expect nothing else." As she started toward the railing, her father said, "Carthenne?" She turned to him. "Your mother would have been pleased with who you've become."

She held his gaze a moment, then drew upon the shadows and jumped to Guya's ship.

———

Book 5 of the Shadow Accords: Shadow Cross

After surviving the blood priests, Carth heads south with a renewed focus, determined to learn more about the Hjan before they gain too much strength and violate the accords.

They reach Asador as one of her crew suffers from a mysterious illness. Finding answers leads her deeper into an underworld she knew existed but had not expected to find so easily. Now she needs to help not only her friend but the many others within Asador who have been used. Carth discovers there are unexpected ways to counter her magic, and she must first save herself before she can help anyone else.

———

Looking for another great read? Soldier Son, Book 1 of The Teralin Sword, out now.

As the second son of the general of the Denraen, Endric wants only to fight, not the commission his father demands of him. When a strange attack in the south leads to the loss of someone close to him, only Endric seems concerned about what happened.

All signs point to an attack on the city, and betrayal by someone deep within the Denraen, but his father no longer trusts his judgment. This forces Endric to make another impulsive decision, one that leads him far from the city on a journey where he discovers how little he knew, and how much more he has to understand. If he can prove himself in time, and with the help of his new allies, he might be able to stop a greater disaster.

ABOUT THE AUTHOR

DK Holmberg currently lives in rural Minnesota where the winter cold and the summer mosquitoes keep him inside and writing.

Word-of-mouth is crucial for any author to succeed and how books are discovered. If you enjoyed the book, please consider leaving a review at Amazon, even if it's only a line or two; it would make all the difference and would be very much appreciated.

Subscribe to my newsletter to be the first to hear about giveaways and new releases.

For more information:
www.dkholmberg.com
dkh@dkholmberg.com

The Heartstone Blade

The Tower of Venass

Blood of the Watcher

The Shadowsteel Forge

The Guild Secret

Rise of the Elder

The Sighted Assassin

The Painted Girl

The Binders Game

The Forgotten

Assassin's End

The Cloud Warrior Saga

Chased by Fire

Bound by Fire

Changed by Fire

Fortress of Fire

Forged in Fire

Serpent of Fire

Servant of Fire

Born of Fire

Broken of Fire

Light of Fire

Cycle of Fire

20018048R00173